monsoonbooks

SPINNING TOP

Barbara Ismail spent several years in Kelantan in the 1970s and '80s, living in Kampong Dusun and Pengkalan Cepa, studying Wayang Siam and the Kelantanese dialect. She holds a PhD in Anthropology from Yale University, and is originally from Brooklyn, New York.

Spinning Top is the fifth in Barbara Ismail's series of Kain Songket Mysteries based in Kelantan. The first book in the series, *Shadow Play*, won Best Debut Novel at the 2012 SBPA Book Awards in Singapore and was shortlisted for the Popular Readers' Choice Awards 2013 in Malaysia; the second book in the series, *Princess Play*, was shortlisted for the Popular Readers' Choice Awards 2014 in Malaysia.

For more information about the author and her books, visit *www.barbaraismail.com*.

Kain Songket Mysteries
(published and forthcoming)

Shadow Play
Princess Play
Spirit Tiger
Moon Kite
Spinning Top
Western Chanting
Little Axe

SPINNING TOP

Volume V in the Kain Songket Mysteries Series

Barbara Ismail

monsoonbooks

First published in 2020
by Monsoon Books Ltd
www.monsoonbooks.co.uk

No.1 The Lodge, Burrough Court, Burrough on the Hill,
Melton Mowbray LE14 2QS, UK

First edition.

ISBN (paperback): 9781912049684
ISBN (ebook): 9781912049691

Copyright©Barbara Ismail, 2020
The moral right of the author has been asserted.

All rights reserved. No part of this publication may be reproduced,
stored in a retrieval system, or transmitted, in any form or by any means
without the prior written permission of the publisher, nor be otherwise
circulated in any form of binding or cover other than that in which
it is published and without a similar condition being imposed on the
subsequent purchaser.

Cover design by Cover Kitchen.

A Cataloguing-in-Publication data record is available from the British
Library.

Printed and bound in Great Britain by Clays Ltd, Elcograf S.p.A.
22 21 20   1 2 3 4 5

For Douglas Raybeck, who introduced me to Kelantan.

Malay Glossary

Adik Younger brother or sister
Alamak A cry of surprise or alarm, much like 'Oh My Goodness!' in English
Ayah Dad
Alhamdulillah Thank God
Azimat Talisman
Batik Wax print fabric native to Malaysia and Indonesia, usually printed on cotton, and used particularly for women's sarong
Bomoh Healer and practitioner of magic
Borek Speckled
Buaian Cloth cradle suspended from the ceiling
Budu Kelantanese fermented fish sauce
Che Mister, short for Encik
Dalang Shadow play puppeteer
Gasing Kelantan top: broad, flat-topped and very heavy
Hantu Ghost
Jampi Spells
Kakak Older sister. A term of address used for women a bit older than oneself (but not old enough to be a *Mak Cik*) and also

between people of the same general age who don't know each other very well.

Kain Songket A silk fabric interwoven with gold thread in geometric designs

Kampong Village

Keropok Fish or shrimp chips

Kirim Salaam To send regards

Laut Sea

Maghrib The prayer at twilight

Main Puteri A spirit exorcism and healing ceremony

Mak Cik Literally 'auntie', a term of address for women older than oneself, and also refers to the cohort of middle aged women (and above)

Mak Mum

Manja Indulged, spoiled (of children)

Nasi Kerabu A dish featuring blue rice with pickles, fried fish or chicken and vegetables, often packaged in banana leaves for takeaway

Niat Intent

Parang A long knife, like a machete

Pasar Besar Main market

Pelesit Familiar spirit

Sarong A tubular skirt of fabric reaching from waist to ankle, worn by both sexes

Semangat Energy, animation, strength

Silat Malay martial arts

Teh Tarik Literally, 'pulled tea'. Usually sold by street hawkers, it is tea with condensed milk poured from on high into a plastic bag, therefore 'pulled'.

Malay Idioms

Gunting makan di-hujong
Scissors cut at their point: illustrating quiet competence and possibly overlooked expertise

Harimau yang tak menaung rajin menangkap
The tiger who doesn't roar often kills

Hujan dari bumi naik kelangit
Rain rises from the earth to the sky: a reversal in the natural order

Jiwa bergantong di-hujong rambut
The soul hangs by the end of a hair. Life is precarious and can end at any time

Karam di-atas darat
Foundered upon land: something inexplicable

Kita semua mati, tapi kubur masing-masing
We all die, but each has his own grave. Each person has his (or her) own fate

Korek lubang ulat
Dig up worm holes: asking for trouble

Macam anjing dapat pasir
Like dogs finding sand (to run in): unalloyed delight

Mati-mati berminyak, biar lecok

If you are going to grease your hair, make sure it's glossy. One might as well be hung for a sheep as a lamb

Membuang garam ke laut

Throwing salt into the sea: something utterly ridiculous

Nasi dah jadi bubur

Rice has already become porridge: no sense crying over spilt milk

Nasi tersaji diluntut

To have rice served at your knees: to have something without exerting much effort to get it

Orang tak berlaga angin

People who can't breathe the same air: people who cannot get along

Pucat lesi macam ayam kena lengit

As pale as a hen plagued by ticks

Putus timba, tinggal tali

The bucket is dropped and only the cord is left. A complete catastrophe

Reba menanti api

The timber awaits the fire: while clearing a forest, felled timber will always be burned. Punishment will always follow the crime.

Seperti anjing melentang denai

Like a dog crossing the track of game: all worked up

Semoga tenang disana

Literally: may (he or she) be in peace there. The equivalent of 'may he rest in peace'.

Tak terasah belakang parang
You can't sharpen the back of a machete: once a bounder always a bounder

Terlayang-layang bagai bulu sehelai
Blown about like a single feather: alone and adrift

Ular di-palu biar mati
If you hit a snake, make sure you kill it. Don't do anything by half

Yang buta mengembus lesong
The blind can blow on the mortar (to keep things from coming out of it). There is a use for everyone.

Chapter I

It was the dry season, when all Kelantan bursts into artistic bloom, with theatre and contests and all manner of entertainment staged in the dry rice paddies, which were now cracked and flat and hard as rock. During the rainy season, these would be seas of mud, home only to water buffalo and leeches, and their usefulness to culture long spent.

A large group of men readied themselves for a top-spinning contest: those in charge of the tops rotating their shoulders and loosening their already prominent biceps. Others, who would watch the tops spin and calculate which had done so the longest, were smoothing the ground to provide a platform. The bettors, always the centre of activity, were watching the throwers get ready, while discussing their histories and the odds.

Kelantan's tops are huge and heavy. The cords wrapped around them are made from thick rope, suitable for the mast of a ship, and it takes strong shoulders and iron muscles to fling them with sufficient force to keep them spinning for any length of time.

Made of metal and wood, a Kelantan *gasing* is about eighteen inches across, with a flat top around which the rope is wound. They hit the ground with a solid thud, and spin with a loud whirring which sets dogs to howling. As with most Kelantan games, a good deal of money rides on the outcome, for without betting, how could one maintain the proper interest?

The men throwing the tops were no larger than other Kelantanese men, nor more obviously muscled, but when they took off their shirts or hitched up their *sarong* to give themselves room to let loose, they were impressive specimens. Their bodies were substantial, since top spinning is hard work, and it was no joke to throw something that heavy and make it spin for twenty minutes or more. They wound themselves up and then exploded with their tops, sending them flying from their hands into an improbably small space. It wasn't just the velocity of their throw, but their accuracy, which many in the crowd found so impressive.

This particular contest was staged in Kampong Laut, near the northern town of Tumpat, on a flat piece of ground not too far from the river, but not close enough to be too sandy for the tops to spin. It was an excellent spot, shaded with coconut palms and a large papaya tree, and providentially, only a few yards from an operating coffee stand. The coffee and snacks so necessary to keeping the participants healthy and hydrated was provided in quantity, and so everyone remained interested, cool and caffeinated, the Kelantan trifecta.

The competitors approached the flat ground, miming tremendous strength and nearly ungovernable enthusiasm; hitching up their sarong like loincloths and adjusting their headscarves. They swung their arms back like discus throwers: top spinning was not all that different except that it was not designed for homicide. The punters looked them over as they would racehorses, looking for well-defined arms and broad shoulders. The display portion of the contest was now in full swing.

When the hurling began in earnest, the tops flew in an arc through the air and landed on the ground point first, spinning ferociously. The men sighed deeply after such effort, wiped their sweating foreheads and watched their tops spin with wooden expressions. It would not do to seem too anxious or excited about the throw or acknowledge the effort which had gone into it. Excited babbling was kept to a minimum even by the bettors, though a low hum, sounding like a swarm of relatively calm bees, hung over the group as they watched and exchanged wagers.

Ramli was throwing next to last, a position he preferred to take, since it allowed him to judge what most of his competition had already done. He was in his early thirties, with the perfect top-spinner's build: strong arms and shoulders, steady legs and excellent balance. He was well known in top circles as a dependable player, calm, controlled, and often a winner. He postured somewhat less than the average spinner, and although an excellent storyteller and boon coffee shop companion, he usually stayed quiet during contests. Those that bet on him, as well as his friends, took comfort in his imperturbability.

Today was no different than any of his other major competitions. He calmly pulled up his sarong and wrapped it between his legs, to preserve decency in the heat of the throw, and tossed his cigarette nonchalantly to the side. He wrapped the heavy rope around the spindle of his top, covering its flat surface, and swung it back and forth a few times to warm up. He twisted his body to get the maximum amount of torque, and then let it fly with a mighty heave. As it never had before in all his years of throwing, it skidded over the platform and scored a bull's eye onto the head of a squatting onlooker, killing him instantly.

The area fell utterly silent for a long moment, as if prolonging the time before anyone would be forced to confront what had just happened. Ramli himself stood absolutely still, his eyes wide but his face expressionless and he stared at the man now falling slowly onto his side, the blood just starting to run down his face. This trickle would soon turn into flood, but in these first seconds it seemed to move slowly, almost as if time could still be moved back a minute or two and have this death unhappen.

And then, the dead man's shoulder hit the ground, and that small sound and puff of dust broke the spell and bedlam ensued, with everyone shouting at once and coming close, but not too close, to the body and explaining to each other what probably caused it. Ramli stood apart from the sound and movement, still exactly where he had been, unable to move.

Someone ran to the local police station, bringing help with him. One look at the corpse and at Ramli, and the officer decided immediately to call the experts from Kota Bharu to handle this. There was absolutely no doubt as to what had happened and who had done it, in a field full of witnesses, but he could already see the 'why' of this murder might be thorny, and Police Chief Osman of Kota Bharu was famed throughout Kelantan as a man who had dealt with murder and knew just what to do. Everyone sat down now and waited for Osman to arrive, while the owner of the coffee shop did so much business he had to send word home for more supplies and several children to help out.

Chapter II

Ramli was born in Kampong Laut, on the banks of the Kelantan River, not far from the field where the top-spinning competition was held. He had grown up there, the youngest of six children, and was therefore somewhat *manja,* or indulged, as people often said of the last child. He was athletic and a natural leader of his gang of boys: choosing up sides in a football game or introducing a particularly interesting form of mischief. He was a handsome and cheeky child, with a happy grin and winning way with him. Ramli was the comedian of the family, the entertainer and, of course, the baby.

He grew to be the tallest in his family, and the broadest shouldered, showing potential in a variety of local sports: football, *silat* martial arts, kite flying and top spinning. In his early teens he began to specialize and found top spinning to be the most congenial, and he was really good. People began to bet on him in contests, and then to support his training regimen. He gained some fame within top-spinning circles.

Ramli did not devote himself entirely to his art, however, but also worked in a lumber mill which had been recently built conveniently in the middle of Kampong Laut. Somewhat spoiled he might have been, but his parents did not extend that to allowing him to loaf around after he'd finished high school. He found a job immediately and began to put money aside for a time when he might want to marry. In the meantime, he drank coffee and remained popular among his friends, and even older men who were always glad to see him join the crowd at the coffee stand by the river.

He wanted to make his own money, and follow the example of his father, one of the few Kelantanese men he knew who were the financial mainstays of their families. Ramli's mother worked selling *budu,* a fermented fish sauce she made to her own secret recipe. She did so without the pressure of supporting the family through her own efforts alone; Ramli's father had strong views about men as providers.

It was inevitable that Ramli would attract the attention of several girls in his village, and even from the next village over, with his athletic prowess and well-paying job. He browsed among them, flirting when it was possible and smiling from afar when it was not, but he had known whom he wanted to marry since he began grade school. It was Keriah, with long thick black braids and dimples on either side of her smile. They were both six when they met, and although it would be far too dramatic to declare that Ramli fell in love in the schoolroom, it would be accurate to state that after two weeks of classes he confided to Nur, his oldest sister, that he would marry Keriah as soon as they were old enough. His family treated this as a joke and repeated it to their relatives as another cute and comic comment from Ramli, but in fact Ramli was serious about it, though he certainly learned after that not to mention it again. To anyone, even Keriah herself.

But when they both went to high school in Kampong Laut, Ramli thought it might be time to let Keriah know that he had plans for them both, and for her part she seemed both amused and receptive at once. She told her mother what Ramli had said, and that she thought it wasn't a bad idea. Her mother nodded noncommittally, and then went to work finding out whether Ramli and his family were serious. It was early for them to marry, certainly, and no one thought it should take place anytime soon, but it was common for people to marry at eighteen or so and really, they weren't that far away from it.

It wasn't long before Ramli's parents arrived at Keriah's home, full of indirect comments and long discussions about nothing in particular, but these were close neighbours after all, and everyone in the village knew all about it almost before it happened. It was, after all, an excellent match: two Kampong Laut families with similar backgrounds, and even the parents of the possible bride and groom had grown up together in the village. There wasn't really that much to talk about, since both were intimately acquainted with the other's economic standing, and neither would demand more than the other could afford.

The marriage was a model one. Ramli and Keriah were devoted to one another, and there was never a breath of scandal or gossip about either of them looking for another partner. They had four children in quick succession, three boys and a girl, the eldest of which was already fourteen and followed his father to top-spinning contests and it was rumoured he might be as good as his father was, or maybe even better.

This was the man who had thrown the top which had killed Hassan, an inoffensive man who was a big fan of top spinning and another resident of Kampong Laut. He was too small and slight to be a top thrower, but he occasionally scooped up a top to set it on the stand to spin. He was fairly quiet though he smiled easily and was an excellent audience.

Hassan had three grown children and was expecting his first grandchild in a month or so. His wife, the mother of his children, was his second try at marriage after a brief and unhappy first marriage while he was still in his teens. He'd been quite relieved not to have had any children from that union, since he felt completely free of it with nothing to ever bring him back to it.

Hassan had tried his hand at a number of sports, including cock fighting and kite flying, but neither really suited him. He hated watching the roosters die in the fights, and after just a few bouts decided he could no longer force himself to watch. He took the two cocks he'd bought to fight and retired them, giving them the run of his yard and the several hens who lived there. This was considered a great joke by the men who continued fighting, but Hassan never cared what they thought; his wife thought all the more of him for saving the birds, who seemed delighted with their new life and never showed any inclination to fight ever again. They would even follow Hassan around the yard when he came down from the house, as if to illustrate their thanks.

Top spinning, however, suited him well, not as a thrower of course, but as an informed spectator. He liked watching the men line up to hurl their tops and recognized their various techniques. And more importantly, he loved the camaraderie in being part of the crowd, the discussions of each man's strong and weak points, the betting and the shouting. He himself was not a great talker or raconteur, but he appreciated it in others.

He knew Ramli, since they were both from Kampong Laut, though he was a good ten years older, and their paths did not often cross. Hassan's small piece of rice land bordered Ramli's father's plot, and occasionally Ramli saw him when he was out helping with the planting or harvest. They'd been polite to each other, certainly, as befits neighbours, but no more. Ramli's oldest brother, Awang, was closer in age to Hassan, and they'd been at school together, but had never been close friends.

Hassan's wife did not have the luxury Ramli's mother enjoyed, and like most Kelantanese women, she was the primary support of her family and ran a coffee shop and tiny restaurant near the ferry stop in Kampong Laut. It was a popular local spot, and her *nasi kerabu* was well known throughout the village. In fact, when Ramli and his friends hung out at the coffee shop, it was most often Hassan's wife's stall they preferred.

Though they had lived close to one another all their lives, they rarely intersected except as neighbours, or as owner to customer. Until the final day when Ramli actually killed Hassan in front of a field full of people.

Chapter III

Police Chief Osman arrived about an hour later, by car from the Kota Bharu police headquarters. Osman had come to Kelantan several years earlier from the West Coast state of Perak, new to the state and his position, and badly in need of help. By now, he'd grown into the job; speaking the Kelantanese dialect with some fluency, as long as it was not spoken too quickly, and having grown familiar with the customs of this very different state of Malaysia.

Kelantan was in the northeast corner of peninsular Malaysia and was once part of Thailand. The local dialect still retained a good deal of Thai loan words, and a pronunciation which often confounded Malays from other regions of the country. It had been relatively isolated from the West Coast, which was far more urbanized with large populations of Chinese and Indians. Kelantan remained primarily Malay, and customs and arts which had long since died elsewhere were healthy and flourishing here.

Osman had been assured that Kelantan, an overwhelmingly rural area, had little serious crime, but since he'd arrived it seemed that murder was always either happening or about to, and he'd seen more of it than any ten of his predecessors combined. He was becoming all too used to the call and the arrival at the scene, with witnesses trying not to look at him or at each other and fear palpable in the air. Sometimes he wondered whether he'd brought this rash of killing with him, but his wife Azrina sternly forbade such nonsense, for how could that possibly be true?

He left the car with a sigh, and immediately straightened himself and squared his shoulders to inspire confidence in the nervous crowd watching him. His deputy, Rahman, walked behind him: a local man, he frequently translated and smoothed over anything that might make their work more difficult. Osman smiled at the local policemen standing near the body, though absolutely not looking at it, and introduced himself, though it was not strictly necessary.

'Yes, Chief Osman,' the Tumpat policeman answered, not bothering to hide his relief that Kota Bharu was taking over, and he would soon be allowed to flee the scene. It was hot, dreadfully hot as only the dry season could be, with neither clouds nor moisture to cool down the bright, piercing sun. It was doing the corpse no good either, and the blood coming from Hassan's head was pooling and coagulating on the ground. The officer swallowed hard and motioned toward the body with an all-purpose gesture. Osman knelt next to it, turning the head slightly to look more closely at the wound.

There was no mystery at all about what had happened: everyone here had seen it. He stood up and beckoned Ramli over to him. It did not appear that Ramli had even moved since he had thrown the lethal top, nor had he spoken. Osman surmised he was in shock from having killed an innocent man. He walked over to him and put what he hoped was a fatherly hand on his shoulder.

'Terrible thing here,' he began quietly.

Ramli turned to look at him but remained silent.

'Everyone saw what happened,' Osman continued. 'There's no mystery here, except whether it was an accident or on purpose, that's how I see it. Which do you think it is?'

Ramli gulped. 'An accident. A dreadful accident. That's what it was.'

Osman thought Ramli looked and sounded less emotional than many others would in his situation but put it down to the shock of it all – maybe this was Ramli's way of coping.

'This has never happened before,' Ramli continued, wiping his forehead. 'Never. I always aim my throws for right in the middle of the platform and I've never missed.' He seemed puzzled by the event.

'How did this one go wrong?' Osman asked, as Rahman scribbled notes.

'It kind of...flew up again after it landed. It only landed for a second, but instead of staying there, it came back up and hit Hassan. How could that happen?' he wondered. 'These tops are heavy. They don't just take off and fly. And,' he continued, 'the ground here is flat. It's been prepared for this, so there aren't any rocks or sticks or anything lying around where a top might hit them.' He squatted down and brushed the swept dirt with his fingers. 'See?' he demanded of Osman. 'It's flat. There's nothing here that would nick a top and make it take off again.' He frowned and stared at the ground.

'Could you throw it so that it would do that?'

He shook his head absentmindedly. 'How? They're too heavy to fly. They come down and they skitter around, maybe, before they really start spinning, but they can't come up. Try this,' he ordered Osman, picking up one of the tops which had been placed among the spectators. 'Just see what it feels like.'

Osman did, and was shocked by just how solid it was. True, he hadn't been practicing so of course he wasn't ready to sling it anywhere, but he quickly brought his other hand forward to help hold it. He couldn't imagine walking around with it, less imagine himself throwing it. 'Heavy,' he agreed, relieved to pass it back to Ramli.

'*Karam di-atas darat,*' Ramli said softly: foundered upon land. 'I can't explain any of it. He placed the top carefully on the ground and stood with his hands folded together in front of him. 'What would you like me to do?'

An excellent question, and one Osman had no answer to. He couldn't see why he would take Ramli to jail if it was an accident. He had no reason to think it was anything other than that, but it worried him, this death happening so suddenly, apparently running contrary to all known laws of physics.

Rahman reminded him that everyone present should be interviewed, and quickly, before they forgot what happened and began embroidering it. 'I want you to stay put,' Osman told Ramli. 'Just sit down and wait for us to get back to you.'

Osman and Rahman chose the oldest of the spectators to begin questioning, as they reasoned he might be among the most knowledgeable people present. They led him to the coffee stand, which was still doing more business than its proprietor had ever dreamed of. With a bit of shade over him, and a coffee provided by the taxpayers of Kelantan, he seemed quite willing to explain all he knew, and to surmise what he didn't.

'I'm Mamat,' he began, stirring his coffee slowly and savouring this new experience. 'I've been watching tops now for more than thirty years, both as a thrower and even as a judge. Ramli is one of the best, he often wins. He's got a great throw, what an arm! And he's strong, you can see that. He has good technique', he opined, leaning back in his chair and looking up at the sky. 'He knows what he's doing. He's been doing it for, I don't know, maybe fifteen years or so. There's a group of people who only bet on Ramli, they have faith in him. He's steady.' Mamat nodded and sipped his coffee. 'Stays calm. That's very important, you know. Guys who get upset or too excited can ruin their swing or they can't concentrate. Not Ramli.'

'Have you ever seen a top do something like that?' Rahman prodded him.

'Without hitting a rock or a branch? No. Did you try to pick one up?' Osman nodded. 'Then you know. It's not something that's going to take off on its own. Even if it did hit a rock, for that matter. And even if you throw it up, it'll come down even faster. Heavy. You have to know how to control it.'

'And if you make a mistake?' Rahman asked.

'It still won't fly. It's more likely to bump along the ground or bury itself in the dust. If it hit Hassan in the leg, there would be no mystery at all. But hitting him in the head. That's something I never thought I'd see. Not that I wanted to,' he explained quickly, 'and I never want to again. But still...'

'It's odd,' Rahman finished for him.

'It's odd,' he agreed. '*Hujan dari bumi naik kelangit*: rain comes from the earth and rises to the sky.'

'Did Hassan and Ramli know each other?' Osman asked.

Mamat shrugged. 'I think they're both from this village, so they must have known each other somewhat. Of course, I don't know either of them that well personally, you know, I know them from top spinning.'

Osman nodded morosely. This case had all the hallmarks he'd come to know in Kelantan: the laws of nature completely contravened, an explanation based on magic, and a good deal of philosophical musings by witnesses. He'd been hoping for something illuminating, but it was still early, and illumination was still possible.

Chapter IV

Maryam was sitting at her stall in Kota Bharu's *pasar besar*, or main market. She owned a stall in a premier location there, inherited from her mother, where she sold *kain songket*, a silk fabric woven with gold designs which is the pride of Kelantan fabrics, and sold throughout Malaysia as wedding and formal wear. Kain songket was the specialty of her home kampong, Kampong Penambang, which offered this fabric in a row of prosperous and imposing stores along its main street, where the fabric was not only sold, but often woven in the yard behind the columned facades.

In middle age, Maryam was a confident *mak cik*, or auntie, most of whom ran Kelantan's economy as traders in cloth, clothing, fish and foods. The sorority of mak cik were proud of their strength and social standing, and even more important, their renowned business acumen. While younger women might still be under the influence of their parents or husbands, mak cik were independent women, even within marriage, and their ability to earn a living contributed greatly to their reluctance to countenance any disrespect.

Her cousin and best friend, Rubiah, held court on the second floor of the market, where she presided over a huge assortment of Malay cakes, the best in Kelantan, by her own admission. She also provided coffee to wash it down, and the small stools in front of her counter were almost always fully occupied. Occasionally, though, the market seemed to empty out for a little while, usually in the late afternoon, and in that time the proprietors of their various stalls were glad of a snack and some coffee to keep them going for the pre-dinner rush.

Rubiah brought down two cups of coffee and a plate piled high with small cakes so she and Maryam could take a break together and discuss the day's events. Maryam moved the cushion she sat on, which was comprised of folded batik made by her brother Malek in his factory. Kain songket was far too valuable to sit on and possibly stain. She moved all the silk carefully out of the way, where no stray drops of coffee might find it, and made room for Rubiah to sit down and rest.

'How are the children?' Rubiah began, safe in the knowledge that she'd need to say nothing else for several minutes, and then would then be allowed to hold forth on her own grandchildren afterward. It was fair and most satisfying.

Maryam and Rubiah had, to the astonishment of many of their peers, taken part in several police investigations assisting Osman and the police force, or as they would have phrased it, actually doing the investigating themselves with Osman and his police force playing a supporting role. It is possible that Osman himself might have agreed with that assessment at one time, though lately he'd developed more confidence in himself, though not enough to actually contradict Maryam. Both women claimed to be sick and tired of dealing with murders, which they believed had never actually happened in Kelantan before the last few years when Osman arrived, though of course they did not accuse him of actual responsibility for it. But in fact, though the work could be tedious and sometimes dangerous, they both loved the opportunity to use their ability to ferret out the truth and tell people what to do.

It had been some time since their last case, and though they invited Osman and his wife Azrina to dinner frequently, talk had not lately been about crime, which Osman assured them had now fallen back into the usual run of speeding and an occasional brawl, but on when Osman's family could be expected to grow. Azrina had joined Osman in Kelantan from Perak, where their marriage had been arranged to spectacular success. She currently taught maths in the Sultanah Zainab High School and was an additional contributor of advice to Osman on how to conduct his investigations. Both Maryam and Rubiah felt that Azrina had the makings of a splendid mak cik if she continued on her current path, and for her part, Azrina was thrilled they thought so highly of her.

If not for the distraction of their grandchildren, Maryam and Rubiah agreed, they might look for some increased excitement in the form of a new case to solve, but there was no lack of work or excitement at home, so an extra dose in the form of serious crime wasn't necessary. When they saw Osman walking into the market, in the diffident way he always approached it, as if the market women surrounding him might surge together to throw him out, they were both on high alert.

The market was traditionally the domain of women in

Kelantan, as women were generally believed to have better heads for business and finance. Most of the sellers were women, except for some of the fishermen who marketed their own fish and carried large and heavy boxes filled with the day's catch and ice. But the rest of the area – fruits and vegetables, household items, fabrics, takeout food and snacks – were run by women, and men, for the most part, tended to avoid doing the shopping if they could help it. If most people agreed women were better at business, then it stood to reason that a male shopper probably didn't know what he was doing, and unless he had relatives in the market who could help him, he'd most likely pay more than he should. And when he got home, he could be assured of someone pointing it out to him.

Osman entered the market like a man going to the gallows. A bit uneasy, but determined to make a good show of it, and reluctant to show fear. It was a look they'd come to recognize, and in order to compensate him for the agony of coming to the market, they greeted him enthusiastically, and Rubiah slipped away immediately to bring him his favourite cakes and coffee. Osman was deceptively slim, given the amount of cakes he was able to pack away at one sitting. Maryam was jealous of his ability in that area but consoled herself with the realization that when he reached her age, he might well not be able to eat with the same abandon he now showed.

'Mak Cik Maryam,' he began, smiling happily to see her and feeling protected now that he was sitting at her stall. Even if he bought something, Maryam would never let him be cheated.

'*Che* Osman,' she replied. 'What are you doing here? You could have come to the house later and stayed away from the market. I know how you feel about it.' She gave him a smile and moved over to give him some room.

'Have you heard?' he asked.

'Heard what?'

'Another murder.'

'No! Is it true?'

'I saw it myself. The body, I mean. And a strange one, Mak Cik. Not like your usual murder at all. I know who did it. Everyone knows, they all saw it.'

Maryam looked puzzled. 'It was at a top-spinning contest in Kampong Laut,' he began, growing more animated. 'Good competitors too. One of them threw the top and it hit the ground and bounced up again, hitting one of the people watching in the head. It killed him instantly.'

Maryam was astonished. 'It flew up again? Those things are so heavy!'

Osman nodded in agreement. 'I know, but everyone saw it happen. And the man it hit was killed instantly.'

She looked at him sharply. 'Was it murder then, or an accident? From what you're telling me...'

'Well, of course at first it looked like an accident. Maybe it still looks that way, but there's something about it...I don't know why I feel this way, but...'

Rubiah bustled down the aisle with a heaping tray and placed it with a flourish in front of Osman. 'What?' she asked, looking at their faces. 'Another murder?'

'Maybe.' Maryam told her. 'Or maybe just an accident. Osman doesn't know.'

He repeated his story to Rubiah. '*Alamak*!' she said. 'What does this Ramli seem like?'

'Very quiet,' Osman remembered. 'Maybe in shock. Didn't seem to be hiding anything.'

'*Harimau yang tak mengaum rajin menangkap*: the tiger who doesn't roar often kills,' Rubiah said wisely. 'It's the quiet ones.'

Maryam almost snorted with impatience, but in the end restrained herself. 'We don't know anything about him yet.' She turned back to Osman. 'What did everyone say who saw it?'

'They all said the same thing happened: the top was thrown, it hit the ground and then flew up again, struck Hassan in the head and killed him right then and there. Ramli didn't look angry or upset, but I think he was quite shocked at what happened.'

'Why do you think it's a murder then?' Rubiah asked.

He looked down for a moment, thinking about what to say. 'I don't know,' he said finally. 'I'm not sure. But there's something about it that bothers me.'

'Of course there is. Someone was killed by a heavy top flying up into the air. It doesn't make sense.'

'Not just that,' Osman replied, 'though that's part of it, you see. But why? That's it. Is he hiding something and thought by doing it in front of so many people it would seem impossible to be considered murder? I mean, it isn't as though I need to find out who did it. We all know that. So, was it an unfortunate accident or a brilliant way to cover up a murder? That's what I want to know.'

'Does he look like he's that kind of mastermind?' Maryam asked.

Osman shook his head. 'No. But that doesn't mean he isn't.'

'But it makes it less likely,' she said thoughtfully. 'Besides, there are far fewer masterminds working than people sometimes think.'

'You mean there are hardly any,' Rubiah added.

'That's what I mean.'

Chapter V

It was time to get to work, to roll up their sleeves, unfurl their sails, sort their metaphors. Maryam and Rubiah sat with their heads together when Osman left, although keeping an eye on the ebb and flow of shoppers so as not to miss the tide when it came in.

'It's an odd case…' Rubiah began.

'Is it a case at all?' Maryam asked. 'What if it was just an accident, and it well might be, and then it's just nothing.'

'That would be the best thing,' Rubiah agreed. 'Then no one bears the sin for it. It would just be unfortunate.'

Maryam nodded. 'We should go talk to his wife. The man who was killed, I mean. Find out what kind of person he was.' She looked pensive. 'But not now. I see people over at the entrance. Customers!'

Rubiah disappeared upstairs and Maryam assumed her professional mien: pleasant, unruffled, ever ready to serve. She loved what she did and was very good at it indeed. Buying songket was primarily done to prepare for a wedding or special occasion, so people came to buy kind of excited and a bit nervous, especially brides and their mothers, and Maryam was an acknowledged expert in serving this market niche. A mother with two daughters drifted over to her stall, examining the stack of songket she'd placed temptingly in the front corner.

'Nice,' the mother said approvingly, feeling a piece of fabric between her thumb and forefinger. 'Woven here?'

'Kampong Penambang,' Maryam answered quickly and proudly, 'just right here. We make the best songket right here in Kelantan.' She turned to the girls. 'A wedding? What colour were you thinking of?'

The girls looked at her shyly but with great interest. One of them spoke; Maryam surmised it must be the bride. 'I was thinking of…silver,' she said, nodding. 'Like grey, but brighter.'

Maryam did not allow any emotion save interest to show on her face. Grey, but brighter? What did that even mean? She looked busily through her stock as though she had grey but brighter right there at hand and came forth with a very light grey fabric with matte gold thread for the design. Looking at it critically, she thought it might even have a hint of lavender. Anyway, bright.

'Here it is,' she said cheerfully, throwing the fabric out with a practiced hand across the counter to show off its colour, heft and beautiful and intricate design. 'A great colour. What a clever choice you've made!' She beamed at the girl and her mother.

All three bent over the cloth to examine it closely, holding it up to the light and feeling the fine weaving but heavy threads. 'We can go outside,' Maryam suggested, 'so you can see the colour in the sunlight. I think it's just what you wanted.'

The mother and her two daughters carefully carried the

folded fabric out into the sun, where they could judge the nature of colour as to its silvery sheen. Maryam stayed at the stall with a resolutely noncommittal look on her face, refusing to think too hard about what they'd asked for, but delighted when she saw their faces as they returned.

The bride nodded. 'Just as I'd imagined,' she gushed. 'It's beautiful.'

Maryam smiled at her and got down to detail as to how much they'd want. It would be a huge order, or huge for her business, and she had a week to gather all the fabric in the right colour together. When they left, she leaned back against her batik pile, and lit a cigarette, pleased with her sale and looking forward to her case.

***

The next morning, Rubiah's daughter Puteh and her friend were dispatched to look after the stalls while Maryam and Rubiah took off to Kampong Laut. It was directly across the Kelantan River from Kampong Penambang and served by a rudimentary ferry which ran between them. The ferry was a flat raft carrying people, motorcycles, merchandise and livestock, and this particular ride had a large cage with several chickens placed prominently in the middle of the ferry. They screeched for the entire trip, which was mercifully brief, and the women were delighted to leave them behind when they got off.

'Maybe they shouldn't carry animals on every trip,' Rubiah grumbled as they walked along the dirt road which served as

Kampong Laut's main street. 'Maybe they should keep some trips just for people.' Maryam didn't disagree – who could, really? At least the chickens were contained; when there were goats, they were all over the ferry and often looked as though they might use the ferry for an unauthorized purpose. Or even butt someone overboard.

They asked at the lumber factory where they might find Hassan's house, and were treated to dispositions on what had happened.

'Poor Hassan,' a burly middle-aged man told them, taking a break from his work. 'What a strange thing! It just goes to show you that when it is your fated time to die, there's no avoiding it. No matter how strange the circumstances, when your time comes it will come to you no matter what.' He looked sad.

'Did you know him well?' Maryam asked.

He shrugged. 'We both live here in the same village,' he said, not answering the question. 'I saw him every day just passing by. We were in school together of course, kind of the same age.' He scratched his head. 'A quiet guy.'

'Did he have any arguments with people?' Rubiah pressed him.

'Not really. He wasn't the kind of person to pick fights. Maybe a few, you know. Over land and such. The same kind of arguments everyone has, but not serious enough to get killed over!'

Maryam nodded and thanked him and got directions to the house. She remembered the village from the very beginning of her detecting career when she'd visited the *dalang* Hamzah here at his home. It hadn't gone very well and ended with her being thrown down the stairs in front of the house, which was both painful and badly humiliating, and she found herself blushing just looking in that direction. She unconsciously squared her shoulders and vowed something like that would never happen again.

They turned off the main road and down a smaller path, with houses on both sides with wide, well-swept yards and a profusion of fruit trees. It was a pretty area, well shaded and clean. It was clear which house was Hassan's, there was a crowd there, with people in the yard and sitting on the porch. Neighbours visiting the bereaved family, they realized; perhaps the funeral had just taken place. It took some nerve to walk in to a family in this situation and start asking them about the 'victim', but they had done this before in other cases and learned to be somewhat less embarrassed by it. Less embarrassed, but not without the feeling altogether. Still, it had to be done, and people needed to be spoken with before they had forgotten everything and started filling in the blanks with stories of their own invention.

Maryam and Rubiah climbed the stairs to the porch and were attended to by a teenaged girl who delivered coffee and cakes almost before they'd sat down. Rubiah asked where the wife and children were and was directed inside to the living room, where they sat together with immobile expressions, just as Malay tradition advised. Neither very happy or too sad was recommended: it was most important to keep an even temper and not fall into immoderate emotion of any kind. Exhibitions of grief at a funeral were discouraged as being liable to upset one's inner balance and leave the soul open to possession. Hassan's family upheld this rule, they were quiet but not in tears, and keeping their equilibrium.

The two women sat down next to Hassan's wife and greeted her, expressing their condolences and hopes that Hassan had passed into a pleasant afterlife. She smiled automatically at them and nodded, not knowing who they were but not really caring either. Maryam introduced herself and Rubiah, explaining they were helping the police and although they realized how difficult this would be, how grateful they would feel if she would take just a moment to speak with them during this sad time.

The widow rose slowly, as her three children and their spouses watched, and waved Maryam and Rubiah to follow her into the bedroom. She sat quietly on the bed and waited for them to start the conversation.

'I'm sorry, *Kakak*, to bother you on a day like this,' Maryam began, while Hassan's wife, whose name was Rosina, waved away her apologies as unnecessary, 'but we would like to find out exactly what happened.'

'It was an accident, wasn't it? That's what I heard.' She looked at them quizzically. 'Are you saying it wasn't?'

'No, no,' Rubiah said soothingly, 'it's just that the police want to make sure that every detail is looked into.'

Rosina looked at her as though she saw through this answer. 'What details?'

Rubiah looked flustered. 'It's just that it was…so unlikely, you know…such a strange accident, the police think, well…'

Maryam took over. 'It is such an uncommon thing to happen, so the police felt it should be looked into to make sure there was nothing else involved.'

'Like *jampi*, spells and witchcraft you mean?' Rosina seemed to have grasped the point very quickly indeed.

'Maybe,' answered Maryam. 'Do you think there was anything like that?'

Rosina shrugged. 'Maybe. There's some who use magic in the competitions, though I don't know if this would come of it.'

'Did your husband use any?'

She gave them a stern look. 'Of course not. He wasn't participating, just watching. What would he need magic for?'

'Right,' Maryam agreed. 'Then who would have that you could think of?'

She sighed, as though talking to Maryam and Rubiah was hard work, and she might not have the energy right now. 'The people throwing the tops,' she said slowly, to make sure they followed her. 'Maybe the people betting. Those are the ones who always use it.'

'Yes.' Maryam nodded politely. 'Do you think they were using black magic?'

She began to look a bit impatient. 'I don't know. Isn't that what you're trying to find out?'

Maryam moved to another perspective. 'Do you know if your husband had any arguments with neighbours or friends?'

Rosina looked thoughtful. She was a small woman, with a delicate build and high cheekbones and she would have been very pretty when animated and smiling. Now, however, she looked drawn, and pale, which brought out the occasional strands of grey in her hair. She'd been married for nearly thirty years, and to have it all snatched away in a moment by something as random as the throw of a top was more than she could really come to terms with. She could not quite believe it happened, and still looked down the lane waiting to see Hassan come home again. She tried to keep herself clear and present, but it was a battle she didn't think she could win. Nor did talking about it help her, because nothing she or anyone else could say made any sense. Fate had played the most ridiculous joke possible on her, and she could not regain her balance.

She frowned before attempting to answer the question. 'Not…really. I mean, you know what kampong life is like; there are always little spats but they're unimportant, and no one kills because of them. It doesn't make any sense.'

'Who would he have had spats with?'

'Oh, you know,' she said vaguely. At this moment her daughter came into the room, heavily pregnant and clearly worried about her mother. '*Mak*?' she asked nervously, 'Are you alright?' She looked at Maryam and Rubiah as if to assess how dangerous they really were.

'Yes, fine,' her mother answered tiredly. 'Just talking about *Ayah*.'

'What about him?'

'Whether he had arguments with anyone lately,' Maryam interjected.

The daughter looked puzzled. 'Arguments? Why? Wasn't it an accident?'

'Probably, of course,' Maryam began.

Ibtisam, the daughter, was undistracted by Maryam's vague denials. 'If it was an accident, the police wouldn't be looking into it,' she insisted, as her mother looked away. 'You must think someone killed my father.'

'No, it isn't that,' Rubiah interjected. 'It's just they want to make sure. We want to make sure,' she corrected herself.

Ibtisam was not mollified. 'Mak Cik,' she began politely, reaching out to hold her mother's hand, 'my father, *semoga tenang disana:* rest his soul, died in front of a whole crowd. There was no mystery there on who did it. Do you think Che Ramli killed him on purpose?' She continued, 'and if he wanted to do such a thing, a terrible thing, would he do it in front of a crowd of people watching him?'

Maryam nodded.

Ibtisam continued, putting her other hand on her belly. 'I can't believe he would do something so wicked, and…yes! So stupid. It isn't a way to kill anyone if that's what you're planning. I think Che Ramli feels terribly guilty about this, and that it was an accident. He was just here a little while ago! Giving his condolences and his apologies, begging our forgiveness. Of course, we gave it. How could we not?' She looked keenly at Maryam.

She reminded Maryam so much of her own daughters. Protective and rational, able to marshal their arguments and present them well. She almost told Ibtisam how much she liked her and admired her for taking this burden off her mother but thought better of it. Now was not the time, in the midst of their grief. And, she reminded herself, Ibtisam was very pregnant, and she wanted to keep her as calm as she could, even though present circumstances weren't very helpful.

'You're right,' Maryam agreed. 'But isn't it possible that

someone else wanted it done and Che Ramli was only an unwitting tool?'

'What do you mean, exactly?'

'Were there any people there, that you know of, who might have held a grudge against your father?'

Ibtisam sighed. '*Jiwa bergantong di-hujong rambut:* the soul hangs on the end of a hair. Life can end so quickly.' She was silent for a moment, gazing at the floor. Her mother grasped her hand. She shook herself to bring herself back to the conversation. 'Yes, life is fleeting. But my father was a good man. I don't know of any arguments he had with anyone; well, certainly none which would end in something like this.'

'What about his land next to Che' Ramli's father?'

'That?' Ibtisam seemed genuinely confused. 'That was ages ago, wasn't it, Mak?' She turned to her mother.

Rosina nodded, now appearing quite interested in what they were saying. 'They have rice fields next to each other, up near the Tumpat road, and you know what it's like. It's easy to squabble over small things when you're working hard right next to each other. But it was never a big deal. They never really fought or stopped speaking to each other. Ask Ramli, ask my sons – they all worked the fields with their fathers and there was no trouble. Besides,' she added on a purely practical note, 'do you think that my husband dying is going to give them the rice paddy? No, indeed, it will belong to my children. So really, what would be the point?'

'Maybe revenge?' suggested Rubiah.

Rosina actually snorted with derision. 'Revenge for what?

Kakak, there are so many detective shows on TV now: *Rockford Files*, *Bionic Woman*, I don't know what else. It makes us see crimes where there are none.'

Chapter VI

'When she puts it like that,' Rubiah began as they walked away from the house, 'it does sound unlikely.'

Maryam nodded. 'I know. I don't know if it even makes sense to go and speak to Ramli and his family, but I think we have to. To be thorough, you know.'

Rubiah sighed. She hated being out of her routine of home and market and village for too long, but if you were going to be a detective, then it must be done completely. *Ular di palu biar mati*: if you hit a snake make sure you kill it! She was ready to do what needed to be done.

They walked through Kampong Laut to Ramli's house, not too far from Hassan's, and certainly a convenient walk to the lumber factory where Ramli worked. He lived next door to his wife's parents, and no more than two minutes from his own, so family was gathered in the combined yards. Ramli's family was no more cheerful than Hassan's had been, and perhaps less so, since they did not have the catharsis of a funeral to buoy them. The whole family seemed to be on the porches of both Ramli's and his in-law's houses, the buzz of conversation very soft and halting. The children were playing in the front, but the adults were quiet, depressed.

Ramli sat with his back against the wall of his house, with his father and brothers next to him, all silent in a companionable way. It was clear to see that on other days, they might be sitting and talking animatedly, but today they seemed tired and sad. Seeing them arrive, Ramli's wife bent down to tell him that people were coming; no doubt several had come to speak to them in the past days and they were duty-bound to put up with it and answer as well as they could. Ramli was, after all, guilty, even if it was an accident, and felt himself in no position to argue with anyone about it.

They were waved up by Ramli's father, who asked them to sit down and with a weary smile asked them what they wanted. Maryam felt self-conscious asking them more questions, when they had probably done nothing but answer the same ones endlessly, but it couldn't be helped.

She introduced herself and Rubiah, explained why they had come and what they were investigating. Ramli himself sighed and tried to pull himself into the semblance of a host. The coffee arrived almost instantly, as did cigarettes, betel nut and cake. These people were absolutely prepared.

'Please,' Ramli invited them quietly. 'I'm not surprised to see the police have sent someone. I spoke to Police Chief Osman at the contest, a very nice man, I thought. I think I know what you want to ask, but please, go ahead and ask it. I'm ready to answer you.'

This was the first time they'd heard him talk, and they were surprised to hear him so soft-spoken. He seemed as tired as they had thought on first glance, but ready to accommodate them as well, and to explain what happened as best he could.

'I don't know what happened,' he began, as if hearing their question without their having to ask it. 'I've never seen a top act like that. You know what they're like, they're really heavy: metal and wood. They never go up on their own. How could they? You have to toss them as hard as you can to get them moving at all, and once they land on the ground, well, they don't leave it.'

'Could there have been a stone or a branch or something it bounced off to make it fly up again?' Maryam asked.

Ramli shook his head. 'I looked. Of course, I looked because it was the only thing I could think of. But the ground had been cleared and flattened for the contest, and then swept to make sure it was clean. I didn't see anything that it would have hit.'

'How soon after you threw did you start to look?'

He looked surprised. 'I'm not sure. As soon as I thought of it. But I'm not sure how quickly I thought there...'

'I was there with him,' one of his brothers offered. 'I helped him feel over the ground, but we didn't find anything.'

'Any dents in the ground?'

'Well, the one made by the top as it hit. Usually you see that and then it's swept flat again before the next throw. It was a strange mark because the top rose again immediately after it hit the ground.'

'But no rocks.'

'I didn't see any.'

Rubiah took a sip of her coffee and a cigarette from the tray before them. 'Do you think anyone could have removed something before you looked for it? That is, was the whole area now full of people?'

The brothers looked at each other. Ramli slowly shrugged. 'I don't know. I wasn't paying attention to that really.'

'Everyone moved over to see Hassan, to see if they could help. There was an instant where no one moved and then suddenly everyone did,' his brother explained.

'Could someone have picked something up before you looked then? In the press of the crowd?' Rubiah repeated.

'Maybe. I can't say for sure. I don't know. I looked a few minutes later...' Ramli answered.

'Was it still smooth?'

'Pretty smooth. I thought it was. I told the police chief it was.' He was plainly worried. 'There might have been some footprints, I don't know.'

Maryam addressed Ramli's brother. 'Did a lot of people walk over the spinning area?'

He frowned, thinking. 'I think people went straight to Hassan and they were standing on the sides. There were already some tops spinning and people were watching them on their stands, you know. I don't think there was a stampede over the platform. I didn't think about it at all till just now. Should I have?'

'We're just asking questions to find out what happened, and why your top should have acted the way it did. I'm not suggesting you did anything wrong, you know. I'm just asking the questions.'

'Maybe some of the guys watching the spinning would have noticed,' Ramli offered. 'They might have been paying more attention. I can give you their names if you like.'

Maryam thanked him and stood to leave. 'We may be back to ask more questions and hope it won't bother you. By the way,' she said casually, as if the answer could not possibly matter, 'do you use any *jampi*, or spells, when you throw?'

Maryam could have sworn that Ramli blushed, although she couldn't imagine why that would be.

'Sometimes,' he mumbled. 'I mean, everyone does.'

She nodded in agreement. Everyone did. 'Do you have a special *bomoh* you use?'

He shook his head. 'No, no one special. I don't spend that much time or money on it. Some people really do.'

'But not you.'

'No. Not me.'

Chapter VII

'He seems truthful,' Rubiah said, when they were finally on the ferry heading towards Kampong Penambang. It had been a long day, and the sun was already low in the sky. Dinnertime was approaching, and Rubiah was anxious to get back home to prepare it.

'He does,' Maryam granted in a distracted sort of way. 'He doesn't seem guilty either, I mean guilty of murdering him. More like guilty of an accident.'

Rubiah watched the ferry tie up on her side of the river and prepared to hurry off. She was always excited to start a case and then uneasy at the change in her beloved routine. When they left the boat and started down the narrow lane which would lead to the main road to the Beach of Passionate Love, Maryam had to quicken her pace to keep up with Rubiah, though she was used to it. Whenever Rubiah was on her way home her steps became more rapid and her determination came to the fore: like a horse going back to the barn, her husband would say.

Rubiah had played a supporting role to her cousin Maryam for most of her life. They were only seven months apart, the only daughters of two sisters, and had been brought up like sisters themselves since their birth. Maryam had been the livelier one, and Rubiah had been quieter, but really, not by much. When they left school and started working, Rubiah pursued her passion for baking rather than going into the family cloth business, which Maryam took over. Rubiah was a truly inspired baker and her cakes were known all over the state. People coming to Kota Bharu from other parts of Kelantan would often make it a point to bring home her cakes as gifts to friends and family, they were that famous.

Rubiah was more often happy than not to be carried along in the tides of Maryam's enthusiasms, like their detecting career, which Rubiah would never have discovered on her own. At first, she was bemused, wondering how she and Maryam could have pretensions to solving crime, but to her very real surprise, they were quite good at it, or maybe quite lucky. Separately and more particularly together they seemed to have an instinct for interpreting clues, and of course, people would prefer to talk to them than to the police. Maryam more often took the lead, and Rubiah was content with that; Maryam's footsteps often led Rubiah to a spontaneous insight. A supporting player she may have appeared, but Rubiah was often the foundation on which Maryam's flights of courage rested. '*Gunting makan di-hujong*' Maryam often said of her cousin: scissors cut at their point, a proverb illustrating quiet competence and expertise which may be overlooked. The two had been together all their lives, and hardly a day had gone by when they didn't see each other. Life alone without the other was hard to imagine for both of them, and their families, husbands, children and grandchildren were completely intertwined.

Rubiah had known her husband Abdullah since they were in school together. He was a solid, responsible boy who'd worked with his father and brothers tending their rice fields and rubber plantation, which was farther south down the Kelantan River. He was pleasant looking and friendly, with broad shoulders and a solid build. Rubiah and her parents thought they would be a happy match: both were on the quiet side, though not silent, certainly, and both liked the comforts of their home. Like Rubiah, Abdullah was not one to volunteer to travel; even when he went down to his rubber land, he left early enough to make sure he'd be home by dinner. And he was devoted to Rubiah and considered himself one of the luckiest men in Kelantan to have a wife as charming and well-matched to him as Rubiah, and a wonderful baker in the bargain.

This evening Rubiah walked quickly enough to nearly break into a trot, and Maryam tried to restrain her. 'What's the problem?' she asked her. 'Are we running late for something?'

Rubiah shook her head wordlessly. 'I don't know, Yam. I feel uneasy, as though something's going wrong at home.'

Maryam said nothing. She had no such feeling, but if Rubiah did…perhaps the grandchildren, or Yi! Someone hurt, suffering, wanting their mother or their grandmother and she was absent. Rubiah's feeling infected her, and though the two were silent, an unspoken conversation went on between them which heightened both their anxiety. Upon reaching Kampong Penambang they were no longer the well-groomed Mak Cik that had left earlier that day, but breathless and sweaty as they each went to their houses as quickly as possible.

Maryam burst in through the door, gasping for breath, her head cloth fallen around her shoulders, a streak of sweat running down the back of her blouse. 'What happened?' she demanded of Yi, who was lying on the living room floor watching *Rawhide* on TV.

'What?' he asked, startled. 'What happened?'

'Where is everyone?' She looked around wildly. 'Where are they?'

'Ayah is out back taking a bath,' Yi reported. 'He wants us all to go and see Ashikin later...'

'The children! Is one of them sick?'

Yi shook his head. 'I don't think so. No one's said so. Ayah just said he hadn't seen them today and he wanted to.'

She thought for a moment. 'Aliza?'

'What about her?' Yi had been alarmed at first but now was losing interest in a prolonged interrogation regarding each of his relatives in turn. 'I haven't heard anything about her, or Azmi, if you were going to ask that next.' He turned back to the TV preparing to ignore this fuss over nothing.

'Is Aliza going to be at Ashikin's later?'

Yi shrugged absently, already transported to the cattle drive. Mamat walked in the back, wrapped in a clean sarong, his hair wet. He smiled when he saw her. 'Yam, how did it go today? I was thinking we should see the kids tonight...'

'There's nothing wrong?' She interrupted him urgently.

'No, why?'

She collapsed into one of the chairs in her living room,

regretting at that moment she had no daughters still at home who could make her some tea. There was absolutely no point in asking Yi. She gave him a fond though exasperated look and turned back to Mamat. 'Rubiah had a feeling that something was wrong. We practically ran back from the ferry. I was so frightened! It still could be something wrong at Rubiah's though…'. She trailed off. 'Yi!' She snapped a command. 'Run over to Mak Cik Rubiah's right now and make sure everything is alright.' He didn't appear to hear her.

'Now!' she raised the volume. Mamat nudged him with his foot and repeated the command with steel in his voice, and Yi stood up and gave them a long look which clearly whined he didn't want to, but he didn't dare say anything. With a longing look at the TV, he turned and jogged out of the house towards Rubiah's, to check whether her premonitions of disaster were true.

***

They weren't, or as Rubiah explained, 'not now, anyway.' Everyone was fine, and not at all puzzled, because Rubiah occasionally had these forebodings. Even when they turned out to be inaccurate, she reminded them at the next minor disaster that she'd felt it was going to happen, just a bit early. Maryam was breathlessly relieved to see all their combined grandchildren and children were unharmed. Aliza and Rahman came to Ashikin's house to show her parents they were alive and well, after Yi had been to their house sounding the alarm.

He had scuffed up the stairs to Aliza's house, also in Kampong Penambang close to both her mother and older sister. 'Liza,' Yi said wearily, leaning against the doorjamb as though to illustrate the concept of exhaustion. 'Mak Cik Rubiah had a feeling and then Mak caught it and is all worried about everything.'

Aliza stopped stirring a curry for a moment and came to the door. 'Are you hungry?' she asked him before addressing anything else. Yi shrugged and then, upon second thought, admitted he might be, a little.

'Come in and eat something,' she pushed him through the door to the kitchen, where Rahman had already sat down. 'Yi!' he said cheerfully.

'Mak and Mak Cik Rubiah are both crazy because Rubiah had a feeling. I was sent to check on everyone,' he explained in a tone of martyrdom, 'because Mak wants to make sure everyone's alright.' He dug into his curry and rice. 'They're going over to Ashikin's later to check on the kids.'

'Another feeling,' Aliza sighed. She turned to Rahman. 'Eventually, something will happen and Mak Cik Rubiah will say she knew it all along. It never fails. Should we go to Ashikin's tonight?'

'Sure,' Rahman agreed easily. He enjoyed his little niece and nephews, and was always happy to see Daud, Ashikin's husband. A little family time might be fun.

Chapter VIII

Indeed, Ashikin's home was packed that evening, with her family and Rubiah's. Just as Aliza (and everyone else) foretold, Rubiah reminded them that just because nothing had happened *yet,* it didn't mean it wasn't going to.

Maryam was a doting though strict grandparent, while her husband Mamat was a doting grandparent offering no discipline whatsoever. This was especially evident in his relationship with their oldest granddaughter, Nuraini, Ashikin's first child. She was much like her mother in that she was very pretty and very assertive and did not take it well that younger siblings may have appropriated any of her radiance. Both Maryam and Ashikin tried to curb this tendency, which might only become worse with now two younger brothers to boss around, but Mamat only coddled her and admired her without admonishing her about being kind to and responsible for her brothers.

'Wait until she starts school,' Mamat would tell her when Nuraini was particularly difficult. 'It'll all sort itself out then. Besides,' he added blandly, 'look at Ashikin and Aliza and how they treated Yi. He turned out alright and so did they.' At this, Ashikin and her mother tried to freeze him with a look, but he'd had a great deal of experience with looks and was not easily frozen. It was clear that curbing Nuraini would fall to other adults.

Nuraini had declared before her newest brother's birth that she would be in charge of caring for him, though when he arrived, she seemed to think better of it. Mamat was holding his youngest grandchild, Nuraini's second brother Yunus, still an infant, trying to induce Nuraini into petting him, but she seemed impatient. 'I'm putting him to sleep,' she announced, having had enough of him taking the spotlight.

'Your *adik* needs to see his family right now,' Ashikin explained to her patiently. 'We're all here together and he needs to be with us too.' She stroked Nuraini's hair and hoped the child would lose some of the jealousy she showed to her brothers when others, particularly Mamat, paid attention to him. Nuraini had gotten into serious trouble only a few days earlier when she tried to push the baby into his cradle to make her father play with her and had learned if not to actually care for the baby, then at least to act as though she did. She carefully did not sulk or pout but moved away to sit with Yi where the possibilities for trouble were less.

Ashikin had her hands full with three small children, and she worked at Daud's parent's songket store in Kota Bharu as well. Daud's parents often babysat for their grandchildren while Ashikin ran the store, but it was a lot to do, and Ashikin had not given birth all that long ago. She watched Nuraini carefully, willing her to get over whatever delusions of queenship she harboured, for which her mother had little time, and often less inclination, to calmly work through it. She'd forced herself to be quiet and forbearing with her daughter, believing that if she scolded her Nuraini would only become more resentful towards her little brothers.

The baby, of course, had little idea what was going on, but Zakaria followed Nuraini around even when she became angry at him. Daud had spoken sharply to Nuraini when she had raised her voice to Zakaria and took away his toys as punishment for some transgression, and after that Nuraini was more careful, but Ashikin believed, internally unchanged. She spoke to her mother about it a great deal, driven by concern not only for the boys and their well-being, but for Nuraini's character as well. Both Maryam and Ashikin agreed that Mamat had a great deal of influence with his granddaughter and could probably teach her about correct behaviour, but he did not care to, and even when pushed refused to acknowledge it. Maryam promised to take a larger role in keeping Nuraini within the bounds of polite behaviour.

Aliza worried that Zakaria, the middle child, would be lost between the imperious Nuraini and the still tiny Yunus, and she and Rahman took special care to play with him and carry him around. He was just under two years old, and at one of the cutest stages of childhood in Aliza's opinion. He loved roughhousing with his uncle. Rubiah still worried her premonition might be true, and asked after Azmi, Maryam's oldest son, who was not present. He lived where the Kelantan River ran into the sea with his wife and new daughter, Hayati. 'Do you think he's alright?' Rubiah asked anxiously.

Rahman swung Zakaria onto his shoulders and listened to his squeals of delight. 'Don't worry, Mak Cik Rubiah,' he assured her.

'The police in Kuala Besar would call me right away if there was any trouble.' Rubiah looked hard at Rahman, trying to decide whether he was laughing at her, but he looked innocent enough, so she ignored it. 'When can we expect a child at your house?' she asked sweetly. Rahman smiled widely and nearly winked at her but didn't. 'We're working on it,' he promised.

Aliza looked proudly at Rahman, her still fairly new husband, and a real-life hero. Rahman had, with absolutely no thought to his own safety, run down a murderer through the main market in Kota Bharu several years earlier, and been badly hurt in the ensuing melee. Though Aliza rarely discussed it with anyone, she admired Rahman enormously, and considered him one of the few people she knew who had both great courage and the humility not to talk about it. For her own part, she saw little reason to tell him how much she admired him, for it might just go to his head and destroy exactly what she treasured. She hoped he noticed it though, and that it made him happy to have his wife look up to him as she did.

Yi was now carrying Nuraini on his shoulders, and she was making easily as much noise as Zakaria was. She ordered Rahman to put Zakaria down. 'He's getting tired,' she explained, 'and he wants to stop.' Zakaria dug his hands into Rahman's hair to prove he wanted no such thing, and Rahman worked hard to extricate himself from the prehensile grasp. 'Take him outside,' Aliza suggested, with a look at Nuraini. Yi, much to Aliza's surprise, carefully took Nuraini down, and sat with her on the porch. 'Aini,' he began, as Aliza eavesdropped, 'that's not nice. I'm surprised at you, trying to stop Zakaria from having fun. Why do you want him to stop? I'm carrying you around, you aren't missing out.'

Nuraini, who had never been chided by her uncle Yi, looked shocked at the turn the conversation had taken. She stared at him, and her lip trembled.

'Now, don't start crying,' he admonished her. 'I want to talk to you and I can't do it if you cry.' She pulled herself together in short order.

'I thought he looked tired,' she said quietly, trying to look angelic and thoughtful, the perfect older sister.

Yi, not quite an adult himself, was not taken in. 'You didn't,' he contradicted her flatly. 'You just wanted him not to be around. Can't you have fun even when he's having fun? Or,' and here he hit a nerve, 'can you only have fun when it's only you and he's just watching?'

Maryam had noticed Aliza standing motionless by the door and assumed she was overhearing something truly interesting. She sidled next to her and listened with her, both of them exchanging looks of wonderment to hear what was said.

Nuraini sat silent, outlining the design on her sarong with her finger. 'Come on, tell me,' Yi urged her. 'And then we can go back to playing.'

Nuraini shrugged her shoulders. 'I just thought…'. She stopped. 'I wanted…'. She didn't like that either. 'You know,' she began again, 'he's just a little boy. He gets tired.'

'So do you.'

'But I'm bigger than he is.'

'You should take care of him and not want to stop him

whenever he's having a good time.'

'Everyone is saying that to me,' she said morosely. 'All the time. Be nice to him, don't push him, you're his big sister. What about me?'

Yi was tempted to ask, 'what about you?' but decided against it. She was already unhappy. 'You're the big sister so you have to be nice to him. Look how Aliza is nice to me.'

Aliza opened her eyes wide and stared at Maryam, who stared back. She never expected to hear this.

'Aliza wouldn't stop me from having a good time,' he continued, while Aliza examined her conscience and found it wanting. 'You have to keep yourself from being angry at them. Everyone loves you. And they'll love you more the nicer you are to your brothers.' He nodded at her as though this was accepted wisdom which everyone knew. He let her think about it for a moment and then stood up and held out his arms so she could get back on his shoulders. He walked back into the living room, startled to see Aliza and his mother standing at the door, but then walked away with Nuraini crowing and ignored them.

Chapter IX

The rest of the top-spinning audience had to be spoken to: someone must have seen something out of the ordinary. Even if it was only an accident, clearly something had gone badly wrong. Rahman gave them the list he'd put together at the scene, with names and addresses, and Maryam and Rubiah set out to cover them all systematically, with Rahman accompanying them to drive the car and offer official backing. 'Which ones are the oldest?' she asked him. 'They've probably seen the most top spinning and might be the first to recognize something strange.'

Rahman began with those farthest from Kampong Penambang, so they could slowly work their way back home. The farthest was all the way in Pasir Mas, across the Kelantan River, and Maryam was surprised someone who lived so far away came to Kampong Laut to see the contest. Surely there were plenty of contests right near Pasir Mas!

It was déjà vu from other investigations she'd made in the past. The village far from her own, a shaded dirt path winding through it, a small house set back among the trees. The house looked lived in, Maryam thought, a polite way of saying a coat of paint would not be amiss. Mahmud, the top aficionado they had come to see, was an older man, who spent his time pursuing the pastimes he loved – top spinning first among them – but as he explained to them when they sat on his porch, also bird singing and shadow play.

'I worked all my life,' he said, gesturing with his cigarette, while his wife sat next to him listening, 'and worked hard. You know, rice growing and some tobacco, it's hard on your back, let me tell you. Well, as you can see, I'm old now and if I don't do these things now, I'll never do them. I can't work in the fields anymore. My knees hurt and my back just can't take it. She sells some stuff in the market,' he indicated his wife with his chin, 'and my kids work the land. We're alright.' He slurped his coffee and leaned back against the wall, content in his conviction that he deserved his retirement and need apologize to no one for enjoying it.

Maryam nodded understandingly. 'You deserve your time now, after working your whole life,' she agreed. He looked at her with new respect, as a woman who saw the realities of life. 'Top spinning, now. Do you have favourites you think are the best?'

He stared up and thought. 'This Ramli, who you've come to talk to me about. Oh, I know why you must be here, he's good. One of the best. Excellent form and very strong.' He nodded. 'A nice guy, too. Friendly without talking too much. Great arm.'

Maryam nodded, encouraging him to talk more.

'A lot of people bet on him,' he continued. 'The same people also pay for his training, or some of it.'

'What does that mean, exactly?' Rubiah asked.

'They give him money so he has some time to train, you know

throwing and such. Keep up his strength. Although if you ask me,' he looked around as if to see who would ask, and decided they all would, 'nothing like working in a rice paddy to strengthen your arms. Best exercise there is, though of course, it's hell on the back.'

'You need a good back to throw,' Maryam said as though this was the fruit of long thought, though in truth, at no point in her life had she ever given top spinning a moment of consideration.

'That you do,' Mahmud agreed. 'And you wouldn't want him hurting it. It would finish his top-spinning career.'

'Did Ramli every have any arguments with anyone?' Maryam pursued.

'You mean did he want to kill Hassan? I doubt it. A stupid way to do it if he did, isn't it? As I said, he was a nice guy, people liked him. Very calm, talked enough but not too much. I follow top spinning pretty thoroughly,' he said, 'and I think I'd hear if there were bad feeling between Ramli and anyone else. And why Hassan? He watched; he never threw. He never competed, certainly never competed with Ramli. What would they argue about?'

'Maybe about something other than top spinning.'

He shrugged, as though arguing about anything other than top spinning would be waste of time and energy. 'I've never heard anything about it.'

'Are there other people whose arguments you do hear about?'

He nodded slowly. 'Well, you do hear about rivalries. There are guys who throw who aren't nearly as nice as Ramli and they take everything very personally. Very. And then of course they get into fights and feuds.'

'You mean fights break out?'

He shifted uneasily. 'Not often. But look,' he leaned forward, 'you've got a group of men together, strong ones, proud ones. It's possible if there's bad feeling, if *orang tak berlaga angin*: people cannot breathe the same air. What can you do if that's the situation?

'But since I know what you're asking,' Mahmud continued, 'I'll tell you. Ramli wasn't the kind to get tangled up like that. He stayed out of arguments.'

Maryam sipped her coffee prettily, then leaned forward and asked, 'What about jampi, Che Mahmud? Are there any bomoh who are involved in this?'

'Of course,' he answered easily. 'Aren't there always?'

Maryam nodded. 'There are, you're right. But sometimes, one hears there are people who are particularly involved, who are supposed to be experts, people like that who can cause trouble. You know a bomoh who turns to the bad can be very dangerous indeed.'

'Now, you don't find jampi in the same way in top spinning as you do in kite flying, or bird singing, or that kind of thing. I think it's because there isn't as much luck involved.' He was preparing to embark on an extensive explanation, Maryam could see that. She exchanged a quick look with Rubiah, who looked resigned. It was the correct attitude, Maryam realized. There was no point in fighting the length of the coming dissertation.

'When you have a kite up there, or a bird singing, you have less control over it, and so you need magic to try to keep a hold of it. But in top spinning, the thrower doesn't let go until the very end, he has it, he's in charge. You see?'

They nodded. 'So there aren't any?' Maryam asked.

He shook his head. 'I didn't say that. There are but it isn't as important. I've known kite fliers who spend fortunes on their jampi, but you don't really see that in top spinning. And most of it is to keep the top spinning, less on the throwing.'

He continued on in this vein for a good twenty minutes, while Maryam, Rubiah and his wife, who was clearly more used to this that were the visitors, sat politely and thought of other things.

Maryam's attention was jerked back to the here and now when he mentioned a name: Omar. She'd missed what he'd said before, since she wasn't listening, but now she was eager to hear what he had to say.

'I'm sorry, Che Mahmud,' she said as sweetly as humanly possible, 'can you tell me again about this Omar?'

For good reason, he was not often asked to repeat himself, so clearing his throat, he began to say it all again, starting much farther back in the monologue than Maryam would have wished, but she was anxious not to stop him before he came to the interesting part.

'So you see,' he said about ten minutes later, during which Maryam and Rubiah hung on his every word, 'there's a bomoh around who kind of specializes in jampi for sports. There was, I think, some talk a year or so ago about someone getting killed at a kite flying contest. I mean, not killed like poor Hassan was, by accident, but actually hung. There was talk that this bomoh is the one who did it. He's got kind of a shady reputation, you know.

I've met him, and I'll tell you now, I don't like him. So maybe you'll have to take what I'm saying carefully, because it's coming from someone who doesn't like him at all. He's sneaky, and I think people who buy jampi from him are wasting their time. He's only worried about himself. He isn't going to give great jampi to his clients. He's saving them for himself.'

He stopped to light a cigarette and lean back. He usually didn't have audiences this rapt, and he wanted to enjoy it. They didn't say a word but looked at him making it clear they yearned for him to continue. And therefore, he indulged them.

'I don't know him well; I'm not pretending to. He doesn't live anywhere near here: he's from up your way, but I can't remember the name of the village. Not that it matters, you could ask and I'm sure people would know him. He always seems to show up at one contest or another: kite flying or top spinning or bull fights, you know, all those things here people buy some spells to win.'

He sighed and shook his head. 'I don't get it. Not buying spells, I get that well enough. I would do it myself if I were competing. But I'd buy it from someone who looks trustworthy. After all,' he intoned, 'people who know about magic can be very dangerous if they don't have a good soul. And you can't teach that, you're born with it. *Tak terasah belakang parang*: you can't sharpen the back of a machete, people are what they are, and he's evil.'

He looked around. 'Perhaps I've said too much,' he demurred. 'I mean, I shouldn't say he's evil because I don't know him well. But that doesn't matter,' he contradicted himself. 'I know that much about him.'

'How do you know it?' Maryam asked.

For the first time since they arrived, Mahmud looked reluctant to say anything. He ran his finger along the floorboards as though he'd never seen them before. 'I've seen him,' he said finally. 'At another top-spinning contest, a couple of years ago. Maybe more, I don't know. A young man used his jampi and he actually came to see him throw. That doesn't happen very much. You almost never see the bomoh at a contest.

'Anyway, this boy throws, but he twists himself. A bad throw? I don't know. But I didn't think it just happened on its own.' His wife interrupted. 'Now, let's not say…'

'I'm just telling them,' he said impatiently. 'They want to know. It might be important.'

'Very true,' said Maryam encouragingly. 'It just might.'

He sighed. 'This boy, his arm broke. We all heard the crack. And he fell as though his knees wouldn't hold him up anymore. Poor thing. Crippled. No one gets crippled from throwing a top. The worst that would happen is that you drop in on your foot. Now that would hurt, and probably break it.'

Maryam corralled him before he could launch into a dissertation about broken feet he had known.

'Too true, Che Mahmud,' she said, nodding encouragingly. 'But you think this bomoh had something to do with this boy hurting himself.'

'I do, and so do most of the people who were there. People were angry at him. It was his face, you see. Now, this boy was his client, and when he fell over like that this bomoh looked … intrigued. Pleased with himself, you might say. Not concerned, not worried as the rest of us were. Everyone else there looked shocked and ran to help him. Not Omar. He stood apart, watching, like he does. Looking interested and happy. I ask you, is that normal?

'Everyone there began to notice it, you know. Several of the men carried this boy off, and one ran for the police to get an ambulance. They took him to the hospital alright, but he never threw again. Crippled he is, limping and his arm hangs in a strange way. He can't really work in the fields or anything like that. He's selling *teh tarik,* pulled tea, in Pasir Mas. Such a shame.

'But as I said,' he circled back to make his point, 'we all noticed that Omar was watching and thinking, but not helping and not caring. The crowd got angry and he backed away. In the end, I think he ran, and a good thing, too, because I don't know what might have happened to him. Whatever it would have been, he would have deserved it.'

'People were angry, then,' Maryam added helpfully.

Mahmud nodded, and held out his cup for his wife to fill. 'There's been some gossip about him, even more lately. I mean in the past year or so. People say he's always trying out his magic and his spirits, his *pelesit*. To see if he can kill people with it. He's always been bad, but now he's worse.'

His wife had clearly had enough. 'Mahmud, don't talk like that. It isn't safe…'

He waved his hand at her. 'She's afraid,' he explained to them. 'She thinks he can hear things said about him and he'll punish us. Don't be silly,' he admonished her. 'He's a bomoh, not a devil. He can't hear us.'

She looked anxious, and irritated. 'I've heard he can,' she said to the women. 'He'll hurt people who say bad things about him.'

Her husband snorted to show what he thought of this line of thinking. She turned to him, growing angrier. 'You say it yourself. You say he's gotten stronger and bolder. You told me about him!'

'Now, let's not be too upset,' Rubiah soothed her. 'When did you start hearing about him? I can't say we've heard much in Kampong Penambang.'

'Maybe because your husbands aren't going to contests,' his wife explained. 'All the talk is at the contests.'

They turned to look at Mahmud, deeply involved in lighting a cigarette. 'It's true,' he admitted. 'That's where the talk is about him. He's gotten bolder, more arrogant lately. He's ready to kill. *Turutkan gatal tiba ke-tulang*: he'll pursue an itch right down to the bone. He can't stop himself now. He'll take it all the way to disaster.'

'As long as it's a disaster for him and not you,' his wife said tartly. 'That's what I'm afraid of.' She turned to Maryam and Rubiah. 'Why should he want to talk about it? You know, you talk about spirits and then they appear.'

'Do you think his *pelesit* will come?'

She looked completely frustrated with an edge of fear. 'How do I know?' she burst out. 'How does anyone know where a pelesit might be, what it might hear? Here we are talking like there's no danger to it, like no one has ever died, or been crippled, but that's not true, is it? People have been hurt and there's danger about. This conversation has to end.' She stood up and walked into the house.

Mahmud looked sheepish. 'I know,' he said, 'it sounds crazy. But she might be right, and anyway, I'm sorry about that. I hope

I've helped you.'

'You've been wonderful,' Maryam said warmly. 'And such an interesting person! I could listen to you talk for hours!'

Mahmud lit up. 'Come back any time,' he invited them happily. 'I'm always happy to talk.'

Chapter X

Rahman was quiet as they drove away. 'He can talk,' Maryam said cheerfully, hoping to lift the gloom that had fallen over them.

'Omar again,' Rubiah ruminated. 'I'm glad he didn't put us together with Omar and the kite flying contest. He seems to have gotten worse, though I didn't think it was possible.'

'He's gotten braver because he got away with it,' Rahman said darkly, staring straight ahead at the road. 'He thinks no one can touch him now.'

'What do you think?' Maryam leaned forward from the back seat. 'Do you think he's involved in this?'

'It would be perfect for him,' Rubiah said sternly. 'A supposed accident, an innocent man suspected, an inexplicable death…'

'It does sound like Omar. This is just how he works,' Maryam said.

'I don't like it,' Rahman spoke to the windshield. 'I don't like anything involved with him. I have to agree with Mahmud's wife: I don't even want to talk about it. It could be dangerous.'

'You don't mean you think his pelesit is going to hear you, do you, Man? Surely not. It's a police matter, a crime.'

'I don't know about pelesit,' he grumbled. 'I don't know anything about them. But I don't want him knowing about me, either.'

'Are you saying,' Maryam chose her words carefully, 'you want us all to leave him alone and say it was an accident? Maybe it was, but don't you think…'

Rahman grit his teeth, his growing anxiety getting the better of him. 'I'm not saying that. I want to get him more than ever. I was never comfortable letting him go after I was sure he'd killed Salim. But if he's stronger now, then we need to be careful. Maybe this should be left to the police, you know. I don't want anyone in the family getting hurt.'

Maryam sniffed her disapproval. 'I think we can look after ourselves,' she said calmly, knowing Rahman spoke from only the best motives. 'Omar can't be allowed to continue like this.'

Rubiah nodded glumly and looked out the window. She had a bad feeling about this.

***

It bothered Maryam, and she did not like the feeling. She'd been disappointed they hadn't been able to hold Omar accountable during her last investigation. She was sure he was the killer, but he'd left no tracks. Clever and unscrupulous, she thought, with no morals and no conscience. It was frightening being pitted against someone like that; he was a dangerous adversary and moreover, he was a skilled if morally contemptible bomoh. Nevertheless, she could not merely sit at home lamenting the fate that had brought

Omar back into her thoughts. If she was going to investigate this, then she would not be stopped by fear. It could well turn out it was an accident: a dreadful, inexplicable accident which left an innocent man dead and another filled with guilt. Or it could be something else.

They had only seen Mahmud of the men present at the ill-fated contest. After the torrent of words, and hearing that Omar was back in their orbit, they had no further energy to continue their interviews. But now, it was another day, and time to get back to work. They couldn't be scared off like schoolchildren.

Rubiah, on the other hand, would have been more than happy to leave the investigation where it now lay, declare it was an accident and walk away. It was wrong, she knew, but her premonitions of disaster depleted her, and she hated tangling once more with black magic and heaven alone knew what else. However, there was no way she could allow Maryam to continue on her own; she'd made a commitment, and she would see this through. But she'd do it with great trepidation and wasn't sure she'd even be able to face seeing Omar again. He made her skin crawl.

She pulled herself together. *Mati-mati berminyak, biar lecok*: if you're going to grease your hair, make it glossy. There would be no half-way measures.

Aliza had her own plans to join her mother and aunt in the investigation. She knew she was the logical heir to detecting, and it fascinated her. Maryam was both delighted to have her along, and uneasy lest Aliza be hurt in any way. Knowing her daughter as she did, she realized it would be impossible to keep her from it once she had made up her mind.

After school the next day, Aliza hurried back to her mother's house, breathless that they might have left without her. Rahman picked them up and they drove off to their next witness—victim, Aliza called it—who was mercifully closer, in Wakaf Bharu, right across the bridge from Kota Bharu. It was a market town, and busy, which made Maryam and Rubiah feel at home. The market was their métier.

They walked down a small street snaking off from the stalls, to a house from which you could still both see and hear the market in full swing. A man was working on the porch organizing large pots of rice and curries, tying them up in preparation to bringing them out for sale.

'Che...Noh,' she called, surreptitiously checking her list of witnesses. He turned around, polite but clearly involved in doing something else and anxious to get on with it.

'Yes,' he said briefly.

They introduced themselves and he looked over the four of them. 'Quite a crowd for the police,' he commented. Rahman stepped forward, giving his name and rank. 'They are helping the police,' he explained, motioning towards them and giving his kinship connection to each.

'It's a family business, I see,' he said, tightening the last knot over the pots. 'You want to talk to me?'

Rahman nodded. 'Fine,' said Noh. 'First you have to help me bring this stuff over there,' he indicated the market with his chin. 'My wife's selling food and I've got to get it over now.' He tied three large pots onto his bicycle, which he walked next to him, and gave Rahman the last one to carry in his arms. They walked off down the road, and Aliza watched with amusement.

'Smart,' she said. '*Yang buta mengembus lesong*: the blind can be put to use blowing into the mortar. He'll use whatever comes to hand.'

'It's a good thing we came here,' Rubiah said, 'I don't think he could have gotten four pots on that bike.'

'Maybe we can start cooking?' Maryam asked. 'I hate to sit around doing nothing.'

'Make yourself useful,' Rubiah admonished her. 'We can sweep the yard.'

Noh and Rahman reappeared almost momentarily, relieved of their burdens. Noh invited them onto the porch to sit and passed around cigarettes. 'Sorry,' he told them. 'My wife's not here. Would you like some coffee? I'd be happy to go and get some,' he said uncertainly.

'Of course not!' Rubiah said. 'Don't trouble yourself. We're fine.'

'Unless you would like something, Che Noh,' Aliza said politely, as the youngest person there. 'I can easily go...'

'No, of course not,' he assured her. The formal dance now being done, they could get down to business.

'So, you want to ask me about the top spinning. I've never seen anything like it. Unbelievable. Like an evil spell made it happen.'

Rubiah gave a start. Here it was again: black magic, evil spells. Couldn't anyone just get murdered or have an accident where the supernatural wasn't invoked?

Noh noticed her jump. 'Are you alright? No, I just meant, it's so…unlikely. Impossible. Inexplicable, that's what it is. These tops don't just jump right up back into the air. They're so heavy. If you dropped one on a rock, I think the rock would break, not the top. And this one flies like a bird. An accursed bird.'

Rubiah nodded, willing herself not to look uneasy.

'Do you know Ramli?' Rahman asked.

'Not well, no. But I see him at contests. I threw a lot when I was younger. Not so much now. It's a young man's profession. After you're older you can put your shoulder out in a moment heaving that thing around.' He drew on his cigarette. 'But I like watching. Ramli is one of the best young guys. Very steady, very strong. And he has a good arm. Lovely form.' He looked at Rahman, not expecting any of the women to know anything about top spinning. And indeed, Maryam reflected to herself, they knew nothing and cared less.

'He seems a nice fellow,' he continued. 'Never seen him in fights with anyone, no arguments, no gossip about him, except about his arm, you know. Friendly guy, easy to talk to. He's funny, a good companion at the contest.'

'Hassan?' Rahman continued.

'I talked to him more,' Noh admitted. 'He doesn't throw either, just a fan. I saw him at a lot of contests and sat with him sometimes. Very knowledgeable. Kind of quiet. Nice guy also.'

'Were you sitting near him when it happened?' Maryam asked.

He shrugged. 'Not far. But let me tell you, that top went straight for him, like a missile.'

'Have you heard of a bomoh named Omar?' Maryam asked. She could feel rather than see Rubiah gritting her teeth.

Noh looked rather startled. 'Omar? Does he have something to do with this?' he demanded.

'I don't know,' Maryam said, shaken. 'That's why I'm asking.'

'That…guy,' he said, remembering there were ladies present. 'I've heard stories about him. At contests. He has jampi for all these things, and he tries them out and people get hurt. I stay away from him. Don't even like talking about him.'

'I understand,' Maryam said. 'But was he there?'

'I don't think so. If he had been everyone would have been talking about it.'

'Could he have been there, and no one saw him? Hiding?'

'How would I know that?' Noh said testily. 'If he were hiding I wouldn't have seen him.'

'True,' Maryam acknowledged.

Noh began to shoot significant looks into the house, and Maryam surmised he had other work to do. They stood, offering their thanks for his help, and left as he went back to work.

Chapter XI

Aliza and Rahman came slowly into Maryam's house the next evening, before dinner was ready. They looked drawn, and though Rahman looked protective and determined, fear was not far from the surface.

'What happened?' Mamat asked anxiously, looking up from his newspaper. He wasn't used to seeing either of them look so glum. 'Are you alright?'

'Where's Mak?' Aliza said, sitting down on the couch.

'Cooking,' said Mamat, and called out 'Yam, Aliza and Rahman are here!'

Maryam bustled out of the kitchen looking pleased. 'Here for dinner? How nice! How is…'. She saw their faces. 'What?'

Rahman began. 'Che Mahmud is dead.'

Maryam fell into a chair. 'What? When?'

'They called me from Pasir Mas,' he explained. 'The police there knew we'd been down there and thought I'd be interested.' He looked exhausted. 'An accident they said. He fell off the stairs to his house and broke his neck. He died immediately.'

Maryam didn't seem to be able to process it exactly. 'Yi, go and get Mak Cik Rubiah right now.' He leapt out the door. 'He fell off the stairs of his own house?'

Rahman nodded.

'That doesn't make any sense,' she said slowly. She turned to Mamat. 'He went up and down those stairs every day. We were just there, they weren't broken or anything. How would he just fall off?'

Mamat looked thoughtful. Maryam had told him all about Omar and the fear he inspired. 'His poor wife,' he began.

'She told him not to talk about it,' Rahman said, clearly feeling guilty. 'She told him it would bring evil.'

'Surely you don't think this is magic?' Mamat asked. 'It's an accident. These things happen.'

'It's a strange accident,' Aliza said.

'Not you!' Mamat said. 'You were always the scholar! You let other people worry about magic and all that. You looked for logic!'

'I know,' she said, twisting in her seat. 'You're right, Ayah. But this just looks so bad.'

'Too much talk about magic,' Mamat said firmly. 'Now you're thinking about it all the time on this. Forget about that,' he instructed her. 'You look for facts. It's easy enough to say magic and then have your reason. It's lazy. Magic doesn't explain everything.'

Aliza looked abashed. 'You're right, Ayah,' she muttered. She knew he was right, but then, thinking about Omar and what Rahman had told her…

Rubiah walked in quickly followed by Yi on her heels. 'What is it? What happened?'

'Che Mahmud is dead,' Maryam told her.

Rubiah paled. 'I knew it. I knew something horrible was going to happen. His wife said so, didn't she? She knew it was going to happen.' She began twisting her hands.

'No one knew anything was going to happen,' Mamat insisted, feeling as though he was fighting against an overpowering tide. 'Why are you all so ready to believe this one man has all this power? That he is Satan himself. I can't believe it! Smart people, all of you, sitting here frightened because you think one man can kill whoever he wants without even being there. His pelesit? Am I really hearing this?'

He looked around the room and realized he was indeed really hearing this. He didn't seem to be getting through to anyone. 'Maryam,' he said desperately, 'listen to me. Do you really think he has spirits running all around Kelantan, from Kampong Laut to Pasir Mas and everywhere else? Don't you think it's more likely there's an explanation to all this, a logical explanation?'

'He's killed before,' Maryam answered slowly. 'He killed Salim, though we could never prove it. And that boy at the top-spinning contest he crippled.' Mamat snorted in frustration. 'And now…'

'Wait a minute,' Mamat advised her. 'You have no idea what happened to Mahmud. People fall, Yam. They aren't necessarily pushed by a spirit. You know that.'

'You're right,' she agreed with no enthusiasm whatsoever. 'We really don't know what happened with Che Mahmud.'

'You're right,' Rahman agreed loudly. 'I'll call the Pasir Mas guys and ask them to find out more. Thank you, Ayah,' he said to

Mamat. 'You've got us back on the right track again. I'm grateful.' Mamat clapped his son-in-law on the back and told him it was his pleasure, and he'd help any way he could. 'I'll go with you to Pasir Mas if you want,' he said cheerfully.

'I only hope he doesn't come after us now,' Rubiah said unhappily. 'He's gotten worse now.'

'You don't know that,' Mamat rebuked her sharply, something he very rarely did. 'You give him all this power. Why? The more you fear him the happier he is, Rubiah.'

'That's true,' Rahman agreed manfully, with a meaningful look to Aliza. 'If you fear him, you work for him.'

Aliza was not feeling half so confident as her husband and father both sounded, but one had to make a stand for science and a natural, rather than supernatural, explanation. 'I think so too, Mak Cik Rubiah,' she agreed, louder than she'd meant to speak, but it resonated with conviction. 'We're the detectives. We can't agree that Omar did it and then be afraid of him. We don't even know if anyone did anything, do we?'

Rubiah continued to look troubled but said nothing. She said quietly to Maryam, 'We'll keep going. Maybe we should even go to see this Omar and stand up to him.'

Maryam nodded. 'I'll take you,' Rahman volunteered.

'I'm going too,' Mamat echoed. 'We'll frighten him!'

Rubiah looked wry, as though she believed this was a mistake but had to go along with it. She could see how the men were trying, and she didn't want to discourage them. Or herself, for that matter. But she believed there was no help for it, and they'd have to confront Omar, and sooner was better than later.

***

After a restless night, they started off the next morning to meet with Omar. It began to come back to Maryam now, as they travelled the road to Pantai Cinta Berahi, the Beach of Passionate Love. The main route from Kota Bharu to the coast was flanked throughout its length with villages and fields. She remembered meeting Omar here before, though she'd done her best to forget it. After they had been unable to charge him for the murder they all believed he'd committed, she couldn't bear to think about it anymore. It offended her sense of justice to think of this man wandering free, able to continue his foul work and the law unable to do anything about it. Maybe this time they'd be luckier.

Near Cabang Tiga, a crossroads for traffic, they turned into a kampong dirt road. It was an optimistic move which was unfortunately unwarranted, as soon enough it became clear it was not meant for cars, or anything else which could not avoid the potholes. Rahman valiantly managed to reverse back to the main road, to the amusement of the coffee shop crowd, who saw this coming and couldn't wait to be proven correct. They all got out of the car, with Rahman's uniform drawing the most interest. They were barraged with questions, as to where they were going and why. When Rahman revealed they were looking for Omar, the crowd quieted for a moment.

'He's farther down that road,' an older man told him. 'Why are you going to see him?'

Rahman shrugged, not wanting to discuss the case out here in front of everyone. 'You know, we're just following up.'

'It's about the top-spinning contest in Kampong Laut, isn't it?' another man sang out. 'I knew in the end someone would come here looking for Omar.'

'Why?' asked Rahman.

The man licked his lips. 'He does a lot of work with sports, you know. Athletes come here all the time to get their jampi. It only makes sense you'd want to see him about this...mystery.'

Rahman concluded this was an extremely whitewashed version of what the man really meant, but now that he'd said it, the man looked a bit uneasy and buried his face in his coffee cup to avoid meeting Rahman's eye.

'Do you know much about Che Omar?' Rahman asked politely.

Suddenly, the murmuring ceased, and conversation stopped dead. The owner of the stall said, 'It's so hot. Wouldn't you all like some tea or coffee? Free for the police and their helpers, of course.' He smiled widely, and most of the men taking up the stools stood up and began to drift away. They all took their seats and looked at the one customer who'd stayed, a grizzled old man who'd lost most of his teeth but none of his hair which he wore long over his ears and tied with a traditional head cloth.

'Good way to clear out a coffee shop,' he said brightly when they all had their cups in front of them. The owner gave him a dirty look, which he calmly ignored.

'Why is that?' Mamat asked.

'No one wants to talk about him,' the man said, still smiling. 'People think his familiar spirit spies on people and reports back what they say.'

'Do people get hurt?' Mamat pursued.

'Not always, no,' he answered cryptically. 'But some do. Trip over a branch, or lose their footing in a rice paddy, fall on the stairs. These things can happen any time.'

'But?'

'But they tend to happen after conversations about him, so people are careful.'

'Are you?'

'I'm old,' he told them, as if they couldn't tell. 'I'm not as afraid as I was, and besides, I won't live forever.'

The owner slammed a plate down on the miniscule counter. 'It isn't really dangerous. I don't believe in the pelesit myself,' he stated firmly. 'Which doesn't mean I wouldn't put it past Omar to do whatever it took to frighten people.'

'He doesn't sound very nice,' Maryam added.

The older man laughed. 'You could say that.'

'But people still come to him for jampi.'

'They do. They believe in his magic if not in him. Or maybe they believe in his magic because they're afraid of him. A lot of people just avoid him altogether.' He grinned happily. 'Maybe that's the best idea.'

Rubiah agreed wholeheartedly and wondered why she herself wasn't following this excellent advice.

Chapter XII

Maryam sighed audibly as they walked down the path towards Omar's house. It seemed more dilapidated and more ominous than she remembered it, but that was probably because she now knew Omar and hated him, while before she'd had no particular opinion. Later, she remembered the house as being surrounded by a black, cloudy mist which set it off from the houses surrounding it and made it seem as it if were on its own ill-starred island.

Omar was at home, crouched on his porch, working on something placed on the floor before him. He was dressed all in black, apparently his preferred colour, and was painfully thin. His face was lined, but his eyes still large and bright, and his fingernails were long, with the nail on his right pinkie kept particularly sharp. Maryam shuddered just looking at it. He smiled when he saw them, which would have been enough to bring a faint-hearted person to a swoon: his teeth were widely spaced and very yellow from years of chain smoking, and the entire effect was cadaverous.

Rahman led the way, standing up straight with his uniform trim and official. 'Che Omar?' he asked politely, though of course he knew who it was. There couldn't possibly be two of them.

'Yes, it's me,' he replied, rising like an insect from his crouch to full height. 'How are you all?' he asked, turning his skull-like face from one to the other, the ghastly smile never wavering. 'Come on up and get out of the sun.'

This was the standard polite invitation, yet to Maryam's ears it sounded dangerous, and she felt as though she were in those horror movies where the victim stands at the door of a deserted house, or a foggy graveyard, and the spectators want to call out 'Don't go in there!' And here she was, climbing the stairs anyway.

'My wife is out,' he said quietly, 'but I can send someone to get some coffee…'

'No need,' Maryam assured him, 'we've just had some. Don't trouble yourself.' And don't poison us, she thought to herself. She knew she needed to stop this or the whole interview would be useless. She cleared her throat and started talking.

'Well, it's been a while, Che Omar, and we were wondering…'

'Yes,' he drawled.

'You seem to know so many athletes: kite flyers and top throwers and all that, and they all come to you for jampi since they know you're an expert,' she explained, clearing her throat. 'As you know, there was a terrible accident at a top-spinning contest in Kampong Laut not very long ago…'

'I heard,' he said, managing to make that innocent statement sound like a threat.

'And I wondered whether you knew any of the people involved.'

'Who was involved?' he asked, disingenuously, she was sure.

'Che Ramli, he was throwing,' she continued. 'And of course,

Che Hassan, he was killed.'

'An accident, you say?'

'Do you know them?' She was getting impatient with his style.

'I've heard of Ramli of course. Hassan, now, I'm not sure.'

'He was a fan,' Rahman told him. 'Not a player, really.'

Omar nodded, saying nothing.

'How do you know Ramli? Has he ever come to you for jampi?' Maryam asked, irritation taking over from fear, which was an improvement.

'Not really. No wait. Maybe he did a while ago. He wasn't a customer; I think he liked the idea of doing it on his own. I don't know for sure, of course, but I don't think he went to other bomoh either, though I could be wrong about that. But again, this was several years ago. Hassan, I don't know him.'

'Did he ever come for jampi?' Rahman asked sternly.

'I don't know him,' Omar repeated. 'I guess not.'

'Do you remember everyone who comes for jampi?'

He smiled again. It was terrible to see. 'Mostly I do. I take my jampi very seriously.'

'Were you experimenting with any top-spinning jampi?' Rahman asked. Omar had killed before, Rahman was pretty sure, experimenting with his spells for kite flying.

'Well now,' he leaned back against the wall with his knees bent. Everything he did or say made Maryam more annoyed. 'I always experiment with jampi. How else can I improve them? I can't just keep doing the same thing all the time without thinking about it. Yes, I think I'm working on some spells which will be better than any others you can get.'

'For top spinning?'

'For everything. Why are you really here? Have you been gossiping about me? Have you heard tales about me?' He shook his head sadly. 'I'm aware of the gossip, you know, all the talk and well, sometimes criticism. I don't like it. I don't like anyone saying things about me which aren't true.'

'And?' Maryam asked.

'And I don't like it. And when I find out about it, and everyone always finds out about things like this, I want to make sure it stops.'

'Are you threatening me?' Rahman asked, getting angry now.

'Of course not. I wouldn't dare threaten the police. No, not at all. I'm simply explaining to you how I feel.'

'Did Ramli talk about you?'

'Why should he?' Omar asked.

'I don't know,' Rahman answered, exasperated. 'I'm asking you.'

Omar shrugged. 'I hadn't heard anything about that. Why? Are you hearing stories about my pelesit?'

'What pelesit?' Rubiah asked. 'Do you have one?'

'Who doesn't think a bomoh has one?' he countered. 'I don't know why you're asking me all of this,' he said, looking grim. 'I feel like you're trying to make me guilty of something. I don't like that.'

'We're just investigating,' Rahman said shortly. 'And now, I think we've taken up enough of your time and we should go.' He stood up, and Maryam and Rubiah followed. As they walked down the stairs, Omar began talking again.

'Don't keep following me around, or talking about me,' he cautioned them. 'I haven't done anything. You're treating me as if I were a guilty person.'

'We're just asking,' Rahman turned and answered, keeping a grip on his temper. 'It's our job.'

'Not to ask like that, it isn't,' Omar said righteously. 'You should be more polite.'

'This is a police investigation,' Rahman reminded him. 'It's not a wedding.'

'Politeness is never out of place,' Omar sniffed.

Rahman was beginning to lose his temper, being lectured on courtesy by a probable murderer and black-hearted shaman. What was the world coming to, when men like that felt justified in telling other people how to behave?

He nodded to Omar and started to leave. He needed no instruction on good manners from the likes of Omar.

Chapter XIII

There had been talk. At first mostly among men, who whispered to each other in coffee shops and at the taxi stands, and then, as always, it was passed on to the women. Maryam and Rubiah had heard it in the market; they were among the last, because everyone knew they had a relationship with Police Chief Osman and were afraid of their reaction. But when they did hear, they defended Osman vigorously.

'I've never heard anything so ridiculous,' Maryam snapped at one of her market friends when she told her. 'Che Osman taking bribes! Never! I simply can't believe it of him, and his wife, I just don't know what she would do to him if she heard. Allowing people to bring filthy movies in Kelantan? No.' She realized as she heard it everyone knew, and many might believe it. Rubiah was on her way downstairs with an afternoon snack and saw Maryam's face.

'What happened?'

'Do you know what I just heard?' she demanded. 'Tell her, Ju.'

Ju, who had a stall close by to Maryam's, looked mortified. 'It's just a rumour I heard,' she apologized. 'But it's all over Kota Bharu.'

'Just listen to this,' Maryam advised Rubiah.

'Well,' Ju began, resigned to her fate, 'people say that Police Chief Osman has been taking money from some of those people near Rantau Panjang who smuggle sex movies from Thailand across the border, and he allows them to be shown. He doesn't arrest anyone for doing it, and they're becoming quite bold.'

'Who are these people?' Rubiah asked. 'Who's bringing in the movies?'

'They say,' Rubiah rolled her eyes at that, but Ju went on, determined to get it over with, 'it's a couple of rich Chinese in Rantau Panjang who are doing it. They have houses right on the river so people can sneak them across without going through customs.'

'They sneak rice across the border without going through customs either,' Maryam reminded her. 'And they've been doing it for years. I don't know if the police chief of Kota Bharu had to be bribed for that.'

'No, you're right.' Ju thought for a moment. 'But these movies!'

Rubiah answered her calmly. 'Ju, listen. If things go across the border, and we all know they do, do you think anyone in Kota Bharu has anything to do with it? Better to look at the border guards on the Malaysian side, or the Thai side, if you think someone's getting bribed. You don't pay someone all the way over here to get stuff across the border there,' she scoffed. 'Even I know that.'

'Well, yes,' Ju admitted.

'This is just a story to make Osman look bad. I'll bet he

doesn't know anything about this.'

'Who would do that?' Ju wondered.

'Omar,' Rubiah intoned with finality. 'Who else would do such a thing?'

'Omar?'

'He's a bomoh who's being...well, anyway, the police are looking into him and he does things like this. Right, Yam?'

Maryam kept absolutely silent, and Rubiah knew she'd said too much. She too fell quiet, and Ju soon left for her own stall, packing several cakes to take with her.

'I shouldn't have said that,' she said to Maryam. 'I'm sorry.'

'Never mind. *Nasi dah jadi bubur*: the rice has already become porridge, and there's no sense worrying about it. Though Ju will tell everyone. But,' she brightened, 'maybe that's a good thing. It may get back to Omar and that might push him into making a mistake.'

***

While cleaning up after dinner, Maryam casually asked Mamat, 'Did you ever watch those movies they bring over from Thailand?'

At first, he looked confused, trying to figure out what she meant by it. Then it dawned. 'You mean like sex movies?'

She nodded.

'Why would I do that? Is that how you think I spend my time?'

'I'm just asking,' she replied, walking down the steps to the kitchen while balancing plates and bowls. He followed her.

'Really? Of course not. Why is this coming up now?' He leaned against the door. 'I've got grandchildren! I'm too old for that sort of thing.' He paused. 'And before you start thinking it, and I know you're going to, I didn't do it when I wasn't too old for it either. It just seemed kind of strange, to sit with a group of men watching that.'

He looked thoughtful. 'Though, come to think of it, no one's asked me about something like that in forever. Do you think I should be insulted? Does that mean I'm out of the group? I've got to ask Dollah if anyone's asked him lately,' he said, thoughtfully. 'Maybe I should spread it around that I'd be interested and see if anyone still wants me at these things. I don't want to feel I'm being left out.'

He turned and walked out of the kitchen as Maryam shook her head and asked herself why she'd ever brought it up in the first place.

After the dishes were washed, she rejoined Mamat in the living room. 'I'm asking because I heard a rumour today at the market. People are saying that Osman has been bribed to let these movies come across the border.'

Mamat looked up from the newspaper. 'Why would anyone bribe him to get things across the border? He's here in Kota Bharu.'

'I know!' she agreed. 'It doesn't make any sense, but it still makes him look bad. It's mean, and it's stupid.'

'Omar,' Mamat said. 'That's what you're thinking, isn't it?'

Maryam nodded.

'It does sound like him. And most people will hear it and

not think about whether it makes a lot of sense. They'll just be shocked and think less of him.'

'I know,' she repeated. 'I hate the thought of that.'

He stood up. 'We should talk to Rahman about this. And I still want to check these things out with Dollah. I'll be very insulted if he's been doing this all these years and not inviting me. There'll be trouble, I promise you.'

'Oh, be quiet.'

***

Rahman looked abashed when they began to talk about Osman. 'I heard it,' he said, looking uncomfortable. 'But I don't believe it. No one does.'

'Of course they don't,' Maryam said briskly. 'But what do we do about it? It would break his heart. And Azrina? I don't even want to think about it.'

'All the police would rally round,' Rahman assured her. 'Even those outside Kota Bharu. No one wants the police force talked about like that. And it doesn't even make any sense,' he added. 'Osman doesn't have anything to do with border crossings all the way in Rantau Panjang. It isn't even police who do that.'

Mamat nodded sagely. 'Exactly. Do you think it's Omar who started these rumours?'

'He's capable of it,' Rahman said. 'He's capable of anything.'

At this point, Rubiah and Dollah came into Aliza's house to join the conference.

'Dollah,' Mamat sang out, 'come over here, I have something

to ask you.' The two retreated into a corner.

Maryam turned to Rubiah with a sigh. 'It's about those movies. I asked Mamat if he'd seen them and he said no, and then told me he was insulted because no one asked him to go. That's what he's asking Dollah about: whether Dollah's been invited to any of these showings and if not, why not?'

'Look at them giggling,' Rubiah said with some impatience. 'Schoolboys.'

Aliza watched them fondly. 'You don't often get to see them as just friends, you know, instead of fathers and uncles. Look at them! They're like kids.'

'Exactly,' Maryam said acidly. 'Boys. Soon they'll be asking Rahman.'

'Asking me what?' He lifted his eyes from his coffee cup.

'If you've been to see those movies,' Aliza informed him. 'Ayah wants to know why no one's asked him.'

Rahman burst out laughing unexpectedly, upending his coffee on his chair. He sprang up, unable to control himself, as Aliza hurried behind him with a dishcloth.

'Is it really that funny?' she asked him, and he nodded, unable to speak. Mamat and Dollah came out of their corner and looked hard at him. 'I hear you want to see the movies,' Rahman gasped.

'What's so funny about that?' Mamat asked sternly, and then he and Dollah joined the laughter. 'My wife thinks I do,' Mamat chortled. 'I don't want to feel left out.'

'Let's go out on the porch,' Maryam said to Rubiah and Aliza. 'We have some serious talking to do.' With a withering look at her menfolk, she led them outside, where they arranged themselves on the floor to the sounds of unfettered mirth inside.

'Alamak!' Rubiah said, 'it isn't really a joke. Not for Osman, anyway.'

'I hate to hear that kind of thing against him,' Aliza said. 'It's so insidious. I don't know how to disprove it: you can't really present evidence for nothing happening.'

'Besides, it's a clever lie. Everyone knows smuggling goes on across the border, I mean rice and fruit and probably these movies, too. 'People will know that part is true and will they then think Osman has something to do with it? As if he had any control over the border.'

'What do we do?' Maryam asked, thinking.

'The police could help. Maybe they could stop the movies, and say it was on orders from Osman?'

'Can they do that?' Rubiah asked doubtfully. 'Would it help?'

'Rahman could ask them. Maybe if the police talk about it to people: you know, that Osman in Kota Bharu is really taking a stand against smuggling…' considered Aliza.

'Only movies,' her mother reminded her. 'No one will thank him if he takes a stand against smuggling rice. We have to be careful.' She corrected herself. 'They have to be careful. You can't get in the way of the rice business.'

They all thought about it. Rice smuggling over the border was a time-honoured tradition which did not invite any meddling. If Osman would be unpopular for allowing questionable movies, he'd be loathed for getting in the way of rice.

'We should talk to Rahman about this. He can talk to the other policemen…'

'He's going to have to extricate himself from the gang there,' Rubiah said with a look towards the door. 'When they finish amusing themselves.'

'I heard that,' Rahman said, leading Mamat and Dollah out the door. Though they were no longer laughing, they still looked amused and were clearly in high spirits.

'*Macam anjing dapat pasir,*' Rubiah noted: like dogs finding sand to run in, showing unadulterated delight. 'Look how pleased you all are.'

'We don't often get that good a laugh,' Mamat explained. 'It's very heartening.'

'No doubt,' Maryam answered drily, 'but now we have to think about Osman. Rahman,' she turned to him in a brusque, no-nonsense way, 'could we possibly get the police in Tumpat and Rantau Panjang, you know, all around there, to look for movies and talk about how Osman has instructed them to clean up all this? Do you think it would help?'

Rahman thought. 'They'd do it, I think, to protect the police and Osman. Would it work? I don't know. This rumour is so sneaky.'

'Do you have any other suggestions?' She looked around at the men.

'Well,' Mamat suggested slowly, 'we could bring it up in coffee shops and argue about it. I don't know how much good it would do, but it's better than sitting silent, isn't it? And maybe in the market itself, if you were to talk to the people there and make them have conversations about it. When they think about how little influence a Kota Bharu police chief would have at the border, they've got to see it's nonsense, don't you think?'

Rubiah nodded. 'It's worth trying.'

Aliza said suddenly, 'Who are these rich Chinese merchants in Rantau Panjang who are supposedly bringing in these movies. Can we find out who they are?'

Maryam stood up, looking worried. 'This doesn't feel right. We're not thinking like professionals. I think Osman needs to be in on this: we can't do it without him. It has to be official.' She paced the porch. 'It isn't a school project. We have to fight this out in the open.'

Chapter XIV

Osman looked slightly stunned. He hadn't heard the gossip or possibly had overheard some of it but hadn't really understood it. He sat behind his desk and tried to focus.

'They said I'm letting in pornography?' he asked distantly. 'I'm taking bribes at the border? I don't even work at the border. I don't have anything to do with it. How can that be?'

'Of course it's nonsense,' Maryam informed him briskly. 'We aren't arguing that. But it has to be stopped even though...'

'What?'

'Even though it's ridiculous.' She lectured, if only to ensure Osman was aware of the pitfalls involved. 'You'd need to stop the movies but not the rice, you understand that? If you stop the rice, I don't know what might happen.

'No one can stop the rice,' Rahman interrupted, 'but you'd be hated even for thinking about it.'

'Forget about the rice!' Osman showed rare impatience. 'I'm not stopping it. Put your worries about rice aside,' he ordered. 'Let's concentrate on the movie thing.' He thought for a moment. 'What would anyone think I would do that? Or that I could, all the way from here. Who brings it in?'

Rahman cleared his throat. 'I hear it's some shopkeeper in Rantau Panjang.' He looked at Maryam. 'Your husband's friend, Ah Pak, who has all the birds?' Maryam nodded. 'It's a friend of his, I think.' Rahman believed, as did many Kelantanese, that all Kelantan Chinese knew one another, and it may well have been the case. He turned to Osman. 'Does it matter who's doing it?'

Osman shrugged. 'Perhaps…maybe…he could be convinced to stop for a while and let it be known the police were on him. If he said so…'

'People might believe him.'

'Where they wouldn't necessarily believe the police, you see.'

Maryam nodded. 'We can speak to Ah Pak. I'm sure he'd help you after what you did for his son.'

'His son was innocent. I didn't do anything for him.'

'He doesn't see it that way,' Maryam informed him. 'He thinks you're a hero.'

Osman sighed and ran his hand over his face. 'Alamak,' he muttered.

'I'll have him come here,' Maryam stood up, ready to get down to action after so much talk and worry. 'Mamat can talk to him first so he'll know what it's about.'

***

Mamat sauntered into Ah Pak's store shortly thereafter, first stopping to admire the birds Ah Pak festooned all over his motorcycle parts store. 'She's a new one,' he informed Mamat, pointing with his chin to a small but energetic bird in a fancy cage hung outside the front door. 'Listen to that.' The two stood under the cage, looking up at the mottled brown bird hopping around her cage and singing beautifully. 'I got her from a breeder down in Gua Musang. Who'd think they'd have birds like this down there, but when I heard this angel, I had to have her.'

Mamat nodded thoughtfully. He well knew how it felt to want a bird more than anything, and this one was a winner. Both Mamat and Ah Pak were singing bird fanciers, and both competed in local contests. Ah Pak had been competing longer, but Mamat was making a name for himself lately, and Borek, his favourite bird, had won several local prizes.

After the birds had been examined, and coffee ordered from a stall down the street, Mamat sat down to put the situation in front of Ah Pak.

'There are stories going around, I hear, about Che Osman.'

'I've heard,' Ah Pak agreed energetically, looking upset. 'Ridiculous. I tell people when I hear them blathering about it. I don't like it at all, after what he did for Kit Siang. I feel I owe him.'

'He doesn't think so,' Mamat assured him. 'He told my wife your son was innocent, and he didn't do anything.'

'An honest man,' Ah Pak commented.

'I think so,' Mamat replied. Ah Pak nodded.

'So, then I hear that someone in Rantau Panjang is bringing in the movies.' Ah Pak nodded again. 'Do you know him?'

'Of course.'

'Do you think it would help if he stopped for a while and told people he did it because Osman was all over him? Would it save his reputation do you think?'

Ah Pak thought about it while slurping his coffee. 'That's the trouble with gossip,' he said slowly. 'It's so hard to stop it. It isn't in the light.'

'I know.'

'But we have to do something. I won't sit by quietly and let him be slandered like this. It isn't fair.'

'I know.'

He thought some more and finally said, 'I don't know if it will help. I don't think it will hurt, though.' He smacked the counter where he sat. 'I'll talk to my friend in in Rantau Panjang and ask him to stop. I'll talk to the club', the association of Chinese shopkeepers in Kelantan, 'and see if I can get people to talk about how strict Osman is. Maybe it will help.'

'Do you want to meet…'

'No.' Ah Pak said emphatically. 'Best no one see me with Osman at all. Besides, it would be embarrassing for him to ask me a favour, and it would be embarrassing for me to hear it. Leave him out of it.'

Mamat smiled gratefully. 'Ah Pak, I don't know how to thank you…'

'There is no need,' he said quietly. 'None at all.'

Chapter XIV

Osman could not have explained to anyone, even himself, what he was doing there. He hadn't told Azrina where he was going, as he feared what she'd say, and moreover she'd be right, and he knew it. But something urged him on to meet this shadowy adversary, to confront him with what he did, and continued to do, and, he devoutly hoped, to convince him to stop.

He walked slowly down the dirt kampong track, in the dark, though many of the houses along the path had their doors opened, and the bright fluorescent light spilled out into the yards, keeping the path less dim. He could here snatches of conversation as he passed, envying everyone their cosy homes and calm evenings. He wished he was home, watching television with Azrina, or just talking in his own living room, drinking his own tea. But here he was in Cabang Tiga, looking for Omar's house with a miserable conversation ahead of him. And that would be if things went well.

Omar lounged on the top of the stairs to his house, with his wife sitting on the porch behind him, looking quietly out into the dark. Osman had never considered the possibility that Omar had a wife – that someone actually lived with him, presumably slept beside him. It didn't bear thinking about.

Osman stood silently at the bottom of the stairs, suddenly feeling as though he had been expected, perhaps even called here, and it made him suddenly anxious.

'I'm here,' he said, though he hadn't meant to say that. It sounded like he'd been summoned for a meeting, and his mouth went dry. Was that what actually happened? He pulled himself together to exert his own will, not to react to Omar's.

The bomoh smiled, or grimaced, and asked him to come up. His wife seemed preternaturally quiet, and she was utterly still.

'I'm so glad to see you,' Omar said politely. 'Thank you for coming.'

'Why are you thanking me?' Osman demanded. 'I've come to talk to you about your...rumours, or whatever they are.'

Omar seemed mildly surprised. 'My rumours? What does that mean?'

'I know what you've done,' Osman said, suddenly very tired, fighting to keep his eyes opened. 'You've told people I've taken bribes at the border.'

'I have?' Omar interrupted.

'You have,' Osman answered emphatically. 'Everyone's talking about it and it can only be you. Why are you doing it? Ruining my reputation?'

Omar went into the house and reappeared momentarily on the porch with a small tray on which rested two cups of coffee, a pack of cigarettes, and a bowl of peanuts. I was definitely expected, Osman thought to himself. I've been summoned here.

Omar took a noisy slurp of his coffee and waved his hand inviting Osman to do the same. He hesitated, much to Omar's amusement. 'You think I'd poison you in my own house?' he asked. 'Don't let your imagination run away with you.'

Osman took a large gulp of coffee, far too large to be polite, in an effort to keep himself awake and alert. 'Che Omar, the only way to talk about this is to talk about it directly. I demand, yes! I demand you withdraw these rumours immediately, or I will...'

'Alamak! What will you do? What are these rumours? I know nothing about them.'

'I will bring charges...'. He was so tired. He just wanted to go home and go to sleep.

'What charges? What have I done?' Omar was smiling, seemingly infinitely entertained by this conversation. 'Police Chief Osman,' he said softly, leaning toward him, 'what did you hope to achieve by this conversation? Did you think I'd fall on my face and confess to whatever it is you're accusing me of?'

Osman jerked himself awake, having nearly toppled over in front of Omar, falling asleep right where he sat. The look on Omar's face, the silent wife, the darkness surrounding him was suddenly terrifying, and he tried to stagger to his feet. He grasped the railing and leaned on it, willing himself to stand, to get down the stairs, even to the next house where he could fall on the road and someone could rescue him. He fell back onto the porch, his head twisted. Omar bent over him, and everything went dark and quiet.

'Stop fighting,' whispered Omar, hovering over the recumbent Osman. 'What are you fighting? You don't even know, do you?' Osman sensed, rather than saw, Omar crouching over him, crooning his questions, keeping him quiet and unable to move.

He could not have said how long this continued – it seemed like both days and like moments.

Something seemed to change; he was no longer lying down, but he did not pick himself up, and this confused him. He tried to look around, but his eyes were closed and heavy, and he could not open them. He heard other voices weaving around him, not just Omar's but a woman, possibly, and other men. It was too much for him to concentrate. He surrendered to his state and let the world slip away from him.

***

Rahman trotted down the dirt road, which seemed more ominous now than when he had seen it during the day. Neighbours leaned out their doors, curious to see him when he moved past, and although he could not see their faces in the gloom, he imagined them to have concerned expressions, knowing where he was headed and why. They must be used to seeing people coming down this path, either looking for spells or looking to get out of them.

He'd brought three of his fellows with him, though three might be overkill. When riding to the rescue, as he was, he emphatically did not want to be caught short of support when the time came for action. The other three followed quietly behind him, trying to remain unseen.

He stopped at the bottom of the stairs with three other policemen at his side and called up to the house. At first, there was no answer, though Rahman thought he'd seen a flickering kerosene lantern through the door. There was silence within, so thick he nearly felt it on his shoulders, and he felt the men beside him moving nervously. He gestured to them and took the stairs two at a time, crashing into the house with flashlights held ahead of them, which washed out the weak kerosene flame in the corner. The sharp beams of light made everything they illuminated ridiculously important: a rolled up woven palm mat, a tray with two coffee cups, with one on its side, Omar's wife, her eyes wide even in the bright light, looking as though she'd been carved out of stone. And finally, Omar himself, crouched over Osman who was stretched out on his back, eyes closed, motionless.

'Thank goodness you're here!' Omar greeted them loudly; jarring after the silence with which he'd first ignored them. 'I was so worried…'

Rahman bent down to look at Osman, and saw no blood or bruises, and yet he was clearly unaware of anything happening around him. 'What happened?' he demanded of Omar.

'I don't know myself,' Omar remained stooped over Osman's head, his hand on his hair. Rahman was alarmed to see Omar touching him: with Omar's small, thin body and long legs, he reminded Rahman of a grasshopper getting ready to wrap his prey and drag it back to wherever he lived. He wasn't sure that in fact Omar wasn't going to do whatever the human equivalent of that might be, and only his interruption was keeping Osman here rather than…he couldn't even think about it, though it was bad.

'He came here to see me,' Omar continued, looking furtively around the dark room, 'and then, all of a sudden, he falls over, just as you see. Why of course, I tried immediately to bring him around. I'm very concerned,' he repeated.

'Why didn't you answer when I called?'

'Did you?' Omar answered, wide-eyed. 'I didn't hear you. I must have been too involved caring for Police Chief Osman and didn't hear anything.'

The oldest policeman among them inserted himself between Omar and Osman, and with a quick sign to the others, they picked up their chief and began carrying him out. 'We'll see you at the car,' he said to Rahman, watching the stairs carefully. 'Come soon, I want to get him home,' he added, and Rahman nodded.

'Such devoted men,' Omar commented. 'Ready to do anything for their boss.'

'What's wrong with that?' Rahman demanded, his hackles up. 'We want to make sure he's safe.' He turned to look at the figure of Omar's wife, still sitting on the porch as she had been when they entered so precipitously. He didn't think she even knew they were there. 'Is your wife alright?' he asked.

Omar shook his head sadly. 'No, she hasn't been well for several years. She doesn't really react to anything, and she doesn't speak. I don't know what's ailing her: we've been to bomoh, and doctors and everything I can think of. But nothing changes.' He sighed loudly and looked at her. 'Still, she's my wife, I can't leave her, I just hope one day she'll wake up and join us again.'

***

He woke at home, in his own bed, with Azrina sitting beside him. He turned his head to look at her, though couldn't manage to say anything.

'You're awake!' she greeted him. '*Alhamdulillah*! I was so worried.' She pressed a cool cloth against his forehead. 'You've slept for a day. Have some tea.'

She poured a cup from a waiting thermos. 'I knew you were going to see Omar, I just knew it. Don't ask me how. I called Rahman and told him, and we followed you there. Rahman brought some of the other men, and of course Aliza came.'

Osman croaked, an unintelligible sound, which could be interpreted, if Azrina wished, as 'of course.' He gratefully drank the tea. He was so thirsty. And still so tired.

'Aliza and I waited in the car – we were the getaway drivers! It was very cloak and dagger,' she chattered on, unwilling to resume the silence that had reigned since he had come home. 'It was a rescue, and we found you! I don't know what might have happened if we'd come later, or just waited for you to get back. I don't even like to think about it. Has he put any spells on you?' she asked, not really waiting for an answer. 'I think getting Pak Lah over here might be the best thing, don't you? In case there are any jampi against you? You want to make sure…'

Osman raised a languid hand and made a half-hearted gesture for Azrina to calm herself. He couldn't yet bring himself to embark on a long explanation—and wasn't sure he had any explanation even if he'd had the strength, but it worried him to see his wife so clearly anxious about him, and he wondered if he was actually as bad off as she seemed to think he was. He tried to smile, which fell somewhat short, but Azrina seemed to appreciate the effort. He took a deep breath, mustered all his energy, said, 'I'll be fine,' and then collapsed back on the pillow, exhausted by the hardship this entailed.

Azrina regarded him with an objective eye and told herself he probably looked worse than he actually was. There were no wounds or marks or bleeding, nothing seemed broken and everything was where it should be. He looked like a doll of himself: physically perfect but with little sprit animating it. Though with enough rest, his spirit, his energy, his *semangat*, would return.

Chapter XV

Maryam and Rubiah had seen their share of Indonesian horror movies, so they knew what was being described without it even being named.

'A zombie,' Rubiah proclaimed with some satisfaction. 'He's made her into a zombie.'

'Is that possible?' Aliza asked, having given an account of the night before in all the detail she and Azrina could glean from Rahman.

Maryam shrugged. 'Once you're doing black magic,' she explained, 'you can do a lot of things. Think about what he was trying to do to Osman, wasn't he well on his way to becoming a zombie as well? Too tired to walk, lying there not knowing what was going on? I can't believe I'm hearing this.'

'It's a good thing we all went to rescue him,' Aliza said, keeping the pride out of her voice. 'I don't know what might have happened if we hadn't turned up. Che Osman might be finished by now.'

Maryam shuddered. 'It's just horrible. At least he's home and safe now. Is he awake?'

'I don't know yet. I'll find out tonight when Rahman comes

home. But Omar's poor wife. He's had all the time in the world to work on her, and now she's like a statue, Rahman said. Doesn't speak, doesn't even really focus her eyes. There's something terrible going on there...'

'I don't doubt it,' Rubiah assured her. 'I always knew there'd be something horrible with him. There already has been.'

'We've forgotten all about it,' Maryam reminded them all. 'I haven't even had a chance to think about the killing, you know. I've just gotten completely caught up with Omar.'

'It's the same thing,' Rubiah told her. 'Omar's in the middle of that murder, you'll see.'

'You don't think it's an accident, then?' Aliza asked, though she already suspected the answer.

Rubiah sniffed eloquently. 'An accident? *Membuang garam ke laut:* throwing salt into the sea. It's absurd! It's no accident!'

'It could be, we just don't know yet,' Maryam countered mildly. 'It's still to be discovered.'

'You won't go wrong looking to Omar for evil,' Rubiah said to no one in particular. 'We thought so before and now he's back again. It's no coincidence.'

'Still,' Maryam began, and then listed what she considered the most salient facts they had. She held up a finger for each of her statements. 'Ramli throws the top, which bounces off the ground and hits Hassan, killing him. Omar is not at the contest, or at least no one's admitted to seeing him. There are rumours about Omar crippling another contestant on another occasion. Ramli's father and Hassan have had words over their fields, but we hear that happened a while ago and there hasn't been any trouble since.

Ramli and Hassan live in the same town but are different ages and are polite but not friends.'

She continued. 'So, what do we have? An unexplained occurrence. A thrower no one seems to be accusing of anything. Yet, a man is dead.'

Rubiah realized it could be a while until the lecture was finished, and leaned back, crossing her arms in front of her, as if to ward off unwanted information. It was clear to her, if not to Maryam, that this unexplained and inexplicable tragedy could be the work of only one person, and she already knew who he was.

Maryam continued, anxious to be out from under Omar's shadow, and return to the clean, bright sunshine of simple murder. 'Everyone seems to think a top can't fly up because it's too heavy, but it's possible. It's happened, so of course it's possible.'

'Maybe it's possible only because there was a spell cast to make it happen,' Rubiah interrupted impatiently. 'Maybe that's the key to the whole case.'

Maryam sighed patiently. 'That's true,' she acknowledged graciously. 'But wouldn't we do better to assume this happened without any magical help? It may provide a conclusion which will be easier, but perhaps…wrong.' Rubiah refused to meet her eyes.

'Could it just have been a terrible accident? I think yes. It's too bad no one looked at the ground carefully before people trampled all over it, to see if there was a stone, or a piece of glass or something that would have…'

'Made a heavy top suddenly take off?' Rubiah asked sarcastically. 'Even if Ramli meant to kill him, could he really have thrown the top so that it would hit the ground and then fly up?'

'A rock, perhaps, something that would push the top…'

'You're dreaming,' Rubiah informed her. 'There's no way a top does that in the natural world.'

'We don't know that much about tops,' Maryam reproved her.

'We don't know that much about elephants,' Rubiah shot back, 'but we know you can't pick them up and throw them down the street.'

'Why does this bother you so?' Maryam asked.

Rubiah uncrossed her arms. 'Because we're going to waste time looking for something we know isn't there! Why don't we start from the beginning? How does it happen that, in front of a crowd of people, a top is thrown to the ground and then relaunches itself to hit someone in the head and kill him? That's the question. Not whether Ramli knew Hassan or whether their fathers had ever had harsh words in the rice fields. It's all about this: how does a top do that? Is it possible in the real world? And if it isn't, how was it made to happen, and who is capable of doing something like that?' Rubiah nodded vigorously. 'And when I look at it like that, I see my answer clearly in front of me.'

Maryam turned away in frustration, while Aliza watched them both, as if it were a game of tennis. 'Isn't it possible,' Aliza began, anxious to restore peace between her mother and aunt, 'that someone swept the top off the ground? You know, when it landed? Don't they sweep around it when it lands?' she asked uncertainly.

'Not that hard,' Rubiah sighed.

'It might be worth asking,' Maryam said, almost to herself. 'A string?'

Rubiah snorted. 'A string? To yank a top off the ground and no one notices? I can't believe that. Black magic makes more sense.'

'The thing is,' Aliza interrupted, 'we need to return to the man who was killed. Who would want to kill him? Or was he just a, I don't know, an experiment?'

Rubiah nodded. 'Exactly. And who would conduct such an experiment? Omar.'

Chapter XVI

Hassan's grandchild had been born in the short time since Maryam and Rubiah had last seen his family. His mother, Ibtisam, was recuperating at her mother's home, lounging on the porch while the baby slept in his *buaian*, a cloth cradle suspended from the ceiling of house. One of Ibtisam's younger sisters was gently bouncing the cradle and speaking softly to the sleeping baby.

Ibtisam sat up when she saw Maryam and Rubiah approaching and smoothed back her hair to make herself presentable. 'Come in from the sun,' she called to them, and signalled one of her younger sisters to bring some refreshments for the arriving Mak Cik.

'Come and sit,' she invited them, patting the floor of the porch near her. 'It's a long way for you to come here, isn't it? And in this heat…'

Maryam cooed over the baby from afar, congratulating Ibtisam and asking after her comfort. 'His name is Zainuddin,' the mother told her, trying to contain her pride and sound modest about him. 'He's been a good baby, so far,' she smiled.

'But it's difficult,' she continued, looking grave, 'you know, with my father gone so recently. He would have loved to see his grandson. There's nothing to be done, though, it's our fate.' She nodded quietly.

Her mother, Rosina, came out onto the porch, drying her hands on a small towel. 'Welcome back, Kakak,' she greeted them, and sat down.

'Your grandson…' Rubiah began.

'Yes, it's wonderful. Someone dies, someone else is born. It's the world. People say he's a sweet baby. I don't know…'. She added politely, not to seem as though she was bragging about her grandson. 'It's nice to have a baby here again.'

'There's nothing like grandchildren,' Maryam agreed.

Rosina gestured to them to drink their coffee and light a cigarette as soon as the refreshments arrived. 'A long way to come in the heat,' she observed.

Maryam agreed. 'We had gotten a bit…side-tracked,' she admitted, sipping her coffee. 'I think it's time to get back to what happened and find out for sure whether it was an accident or…' she paused.

'Murder?' asked Rosina, shaking her head. 'Ramli? No, I can tell you myself Ramli never meant to hurt anyone. More than anyone, I would want to see anyone who did this to my husband brought to justice, but it isn't Ramli. It's a terrible accident, one we are all sorry for, even Ramli himself. You can call off your investigation right now. There's no murder.'

'But what if it wasn't Ramli,' Rubiah leaned forward to offer her favourite theory. 'What if Ramli was just an innocent bystander, so to speak, and the real murderer was someone else?'

Rosina looked at her sympathetically. 'Kakak, a whole crowd of people saw it happen. Ramli threw the top. No one else. I'm not sure what you're looking for.' She looked strained, and Maryam began to feel as though they were torturing her for no reason. Maybe it really was an accident and they were off into the weeds, solving a problem that never existed. She sighed and Rubiah gave her a sharp look.

'A bomoh named Omar, perhaps?' Rubiah asked diffidently. 'Does that name mean anything to you?'

Rosina and Ibtisam exchanged glances, and Rubiah knew she'd felt the first tug on her string. 'You know him,' she said, trying to hide her excitement.

'Well,' Ibtisam explained, looking at her mother. 'We've... heard of him.'

'Where?'

'He does a lot of jampi for people who participate in contests, you know. Kite flying, bird singing, that kind of thing.'

'And top spinning?'

'I guess,' she answered noncommittally.

'Did your father know him?'

'My father just watched. He was a fan, you know. Not a top thrower. He wouldn't have used any jampi.'

'Did he ever do anything like that?'

'I don't think so...'

'He did,' her mother interrupted, looking even more tired than she had moments before. 'He used to have fighting cocks, but he couldn't stand watching them die. He stopped and let them just stay in the yard. They followed him around like dogs.'

She smiled.

'I remember,' Ibtisam said, her eyes lighting up. 'Those big roosters who'd wait for him at the bottom of the stairs in the morning! It was so funny, Mak Cik! They'd crow and wait for him to come down, and when I was little, I'd follow him down to play with them. It's been years since I thought of that.' She smiled delightedly. 'I'm so glad to think about that again. He was such a special man, my father. Who else had grateful fighting cocks who'd trail him around the yard?'

Maryam and Rubiah couldn't help smiling also. Maryam felt it told her more about Hassan than anything else she'd heard. What a good heart!

'Is that when he met Omar?' Rubiah asked.

Rosina's smile faded. 'Around then, yes. When he was still thinking he'd have them fight. Someone told him Omar had the strongest jampi. This must be twenty years ago at least.'

'Did you meet him?'

'I did.' She closed her mouth as though to ensure nothing more came out of it.

'You didn't care for him,' Maryam interpreted her look.

'Not at all.'

'Why not?'

'He seemed…that is, when I saw him…I don't know what I'm saying. You'll laugh at me, but this is the truth. I felt like when he came into my yard, the sky got darker. Is that crazy? Maybe it is but that's how I felt. He carried the darkness around with him. Have you met him?'

Maryam nodded.

'Then you know. He probably looks the same now as he did, only worse, I imagine. Very skinny, terrible teeth, even though he wasn't an old man at the time. Horrible. I hated him right away and I told Hassan, you shouldn't be dealing with a man like that. It's dangerous. No jampi is worth that, and you know it.

'Well, he agreed with me in the end. When he decided to retire the birds. I think Omar scared him too, but he was embarrassed to admit it. You know what men are like.'

They did.

'But Hassan was a good man. A generous one, thoughtful. A good father, a good husband. There aren't many like him. That's something Omar would never understand.'

'What do you mean? Did they have an argument?'

'No, well, not really. I don't know. I'm not making sense, here.'

They assured her she was.

'You see, the problem is I'm trying to describe something I can't put words to. I wouldn't have said more than ten words to this Omar. But I'm telling you when he left suddenly the sun was brighter. I saw him cast shadows over everything, over Hassan, over his birds. He spread evil over everything he saw, and for Hassan to have invited that evil into his house for some jampi for cockfighting ... I couldn't believe it. Especially because Hassan's heart wasn't in it at all.'

She smoked quietly for a moment while she gathered her thoughts. Rubiah crossed her arms in front of her as if to ward off evil spirits. How had she gone almost her entire life never hearing of Omar, and then over the last two years she heard about him all the time? And when she wasn't actively hearing about him, he invaded her thoughts and scared her anyway. She fervently hoped that she'd spend the rest of her life as she had spent it before: in blissful ignorance of Omar's very existence.

'Why would this guy even have remembered Hassan?' Rosina asked, mostly to herself. 'I don't understand. Why would he have anything to do with it. He wasn't there at the contest, was he?'

'No one noticed him.'

'Oh, they would have had he been there. He's hard to miss, like a skeleton dressed in black.'

Chapter XVII

'There's a guy at the door,' Yi informed Maryam as she sat on the floor of the living room, surrounded by mounds of folded kain songket. She kept up a running commentary on her stock to Mamat, who sat on the couch reading the paper and grunting occasionally to signal profound interest and perhaps approval of any action she'd taken. It was fine with Maryam, she didn't really expect much input from Mamat but liked to be able to discuss the finer points of songket weaving with someone, even someone who wasn't really listening. It's often difficult being an expert.

'What kind of guy?' she answered, not really looking forward to visitors and positively reluctant to repack her fabric. She was right in the middle of an important task.

'I don't know,' Yi answered helpfully. 'He wants to see you.'

'Me?'

Yi nodded, and invited the guy to come in before Maryam could say anything. Ramli walked into the room looking shy and somewhat embarrassed. His wife followed behind him.

'I'm sorry,' he apologized, 'I didn't realize you were right in the middle of working.' He began to back out, but Maryam called them in, rising from her songket and waving them to the couch beside Mamat. 'It's nothing.'

Yi was dispatched to the local coffee stand for refreshments, and Mamat passed out his Rothman's cigarettes to his guests.

Maryam introduced them all and waited politely for someone to tell her why they were here. Keriah, Ramli's wife, began, speaking as quickly as she could to get it over with.

'Mak Cik, I know you're investigating this horrible accident, and of course we want to do all we can to help. Ramli hasn't been able to rest since it happened, you know, he feels so bad about it. He certainly didn't want to do anything like that, I mean, who would, right?' She nodded rapidly, and Maryam agreed.

'You can imagine how we've been talking about it all the time, trying to remember each detail of what was happening. Ramli's brothers as well. We're going over it again and again...'. She swallowed and looked at Ramli, who stirred uncomfortably and began to speak.

'I just thought of something,' he spoke as slowly as he wife did quickly, 'maybe it has something to do with it, maybe not. I don't know. I thought you would be the expert so maybe you could decide if it meant anything or not.'

Maryam silently urged them to get to the point, but her face remained bland and polite, and she said nothing.

Ramli sighed and began again. 'I used some jampi sometimes, I told you, right? I know I did. I'd just gotten one before this competition, and I wonder...'

'Omar!' Maryam exclaimed. 'It's him, isn't it?'

'No,' Ramli looked somewhat puzzled. 'No, I've heard of him but never got anything from him. He has a terrible reputation.'

Keriah interrupted. 'People say he's evil, Mak Cik. That he can hurt you from afar. I hope you haven't had anything to do with him.' She looked searchingly at Maryam and then Mamat.

'I wouldn't use him,' Ramli began again. 'He scares me, I don't mind admitting it. The talk about him that goes on, even though I'm not sure it's all true, but even if part of it is it's pretty scary. So no, I just use someone in Kampong Laut. Maybe not a specialist but not frightening either.'

'And?'

'I wonder if he knew Hassan. I mean, we're all from Kampong Laut, right? It's not that big. Could he know something about Hassan? Bomoh do, sometimes.'

Maryam nodded, a bit disappointed it wasn't Omar he'd come to tell her about but still it was another lead. 'What's his name?'

'Deraman.' Ramli answered. 'You can find him easily in Kampong Laut. He lives right near the ferry landing.

'We'll go to see him,' Maryam said with more energy than she felt. The thought of going back to Kampong Laut again did not excite her, but she would do it nevertheless, as her duty.

***

Maryam looked tired, Rubiah morose, and only Aliza was excited to be part of the team. She looked critically at her mother and aunt, the two strong pillars of her world growing up, and noticed fearfully they looked older to her than they'd ever done. Not that they'd allowed much grey in their hair or failed to dress up to the Kelantan standard. But it was their eyes, she decided, which looked duller than usual, less energetic. The thought of either of them becoming old and infirm, no longer forces to be reckoned with, horrified her. It was hard to imagine a world without these two in charge of it. She began chattering in a move to bring them out of their lethargy.

'I don't really want to go back to Kampong Laut,' Rubiah answered her questions. 'I think we should acknowledge it was an accident, maybe an accident we can't quite explain, and let it go at that. I'm sick of talking about bomoh and black magic and how tops move, and the only reason I'm here,' she began to pick up speed and some energy, 'is because of her.' She pointed to Maryam with her chin. 'I can't let her go by herself and she's so stubborn, no one can talk her out of doing anything.' Maryam watched her but said nothing, and her expression didn't change. 'I don't like this at all, this Omar creature, and what's happened to Osman, poor boy.' Aliza couldn't help but smile at how Osman would feel being referred to that way. Although, it was possible he was used to it by now.

'Somebody's going to get killed,' Rubiah foretold in sepulchral tones. 'More than already have done. This Omar is going to take all of Kelantan down with him, you'll see,' she foretold.

'Then shouldn't we try to stop him?' Aliza asked. 'It's our duty!'

'No, it isn't,' Rubiah contradicted her sharply. 'It's the police's duty. We're just helping them. Two Mak Cik helping out. And you,' she added politely. Not quite a Mak Cik yet – a Mak Cik in training.

'Don't be so unhappy about this,' Maryam sighed and placed a fond hand on Rubiah's arm. 'I think we're trying to protect us all from a very dangerous man, who someone should have stopped long ago, but no one did. Now he's grown so powerful...'

'That we need to go after him? Isn't that what the police are for?'

'We must help.' Maryam fell silent and looked away, across the brown and choppy river, as though the coconut plantation on the Kampong Laut side could be read for clues. Rubiah gave Aliza a meaningful look and stayed silent herself for the few moments before they landed.

Maryam soon found out where Deraman lived and they began walking towards his house. It was surprisingly large and well kept, with a TV antenna and robust geese patrolling the front yard. The lady of the house, drawn by the cacophony set up by her watch-fowl invited them up and began plying them with beverages before they'd managed to sit down.

'He'll be right back,' she assured them cheerfully, clearly used to having visitors, or customers, show up unannounced. 'You just relax and have something to drink and he'll be back before you know it.'

Aliza looked eagerly around, taking in the house and its obvious prosperity, while Rubiah and Maryam lit cigarettes and sipped sweet coffee. As his wife had promised, Deraman was coming up the stairs, greeting them with a professional smile. He sat down with them, and was, of course, immediately served some coffee and snacks.

'It's about Ramli,' Maryam began when the introductions

and small talk were completed.

'The accident,' he said sadly, nodding. 'Everyone knows about it.'

'Were you there?'

He shook his head. 'No, I don't usually go, especially if I've given jampi to one of the contestants. I get too nervous about it, and then I feel bad if they don't win. Anyway,' he continued genially, 'I'm not a huge fan and not that knowledgeable, so it's not as though I feel I've missed too much.'

'Do you know Omar?' Rubiah suddenly blurted out, as if she simply could not wait to get this subject on the table. Maryam frowned at her, but it was too late, it had already been introduced.

Deraman looked keenly back at each in turn and nodded. 'Everyone's heard of him.'

'Do you know him well?' Maryam asked.

Deraman leaned back. Clearly this was an answer which would require some thought. Maryam was suddenly alert, watching him carefully. He lit a cigarette and offered them around, stirred his coffee one more time, and generally avoided saying anything for as long as he could.

'It's...difficult, Kakak,' he finally said. 'I know him. Well? I'm not sure. Now anyway. I used to, at one time, but I almost never see him now. He was a talented bomoh, he really had an...extraordinary ability to connect with the spirits. I envied that when I was younger. But then...well, he changed, you see. I don't know what happened,' he pondered, forestalling their next question, 'he just changed. As if he'd gotten too far involved with what he was doing and forgot about this world and this life. And then his wife got sick.'

'Sick?'

'Something with her mind. She couldn't remember things or recognize people. She stopped talking. As though she were an empty husk.

'Omar was mad to cure her. They were a love match, you see, and he was devoted to her. I think he tried everything and that just got him deeper into black magic.'

'I thought he'd done it to her,' Rubiah interrupted. 'You know, taken her mind and made her a zombie.'

He gave a short laugh. 'That's for movies, Kakak. No, he certainly didn't bring it about. He was beside himself. They had no children, you see, just each other. It was sad. She's still like that. He takes care of her. I hear that every so often she seems to be back, remembers what to do, or seems to recognize people. But it doesn't last long.

'He's really taken his image as a sorcerer very seriously,' he continued, bemused. 'I saw him a while ago. This dressing all in black and his teeth falling out. He's embraced it. He wasn't at all like this before.'

'What was he like?' Rubiah asked, intrigued.

He looked at her for a long moment. 'Like anyone else. Just a normal guy. Now he's Count Dracula.'

'What do you think happened?' Rubiah urged him to consider.

He took a sip of coffee and stared off into the distance, then remembered he had a cigarette going and applied himself to it. 'I think, well, I don't really know.... But I think he just got so depressed he let everything go to hell, himself most of all. People fear him now; I hear stories about him and his pelesit. He's completely isolated now. No one goes near him.

'I understand why, of course I do. He scares me, and I don't think of him as the Prince of Darkness. But look at him! He's a walking corpse.'

Rubiah heartily agreed. 'Even though he may have a reason, he still became awful. People say he knows when they talk about him, and then they die.'

Deraman snorted. 'Really? You surely don't believe that, Kakak.'

'I might,' she said defensively, 'we spoke to a man who'd been at the contest, and his wife told him to be quiet, that Omar would find out...'

'It sounds like a story to scare children.'

'And he died. Fell off the stairs in his own house,' she finished triumphantly. 'He also made a boy crippled at another top tournament.'

'You've been collecting a lot of information,' he observed calmly.

Rubiah shrugged and sat silent. 'Look,' he began again, a slight frown creasing his forehead, 'I'm not defending Omar, I'm not saying anything about what he may have done lately. I haven't seen him in a long time, but I am saying...that is, I'm telling you he wasn't always like this. He was, years ago, a normal person. Who looked like everyone else...'

'Not anymore,' Rubiah informed him, unnecessarily.

'I know,' he said patiently, determined not to be goaded into irritation, 'I know he's like that now. You're right, Kakak. But,' he held up his right forefinger, 'as I once knew him, he wasn't evil, and he loved his wife.'

'It certainly does give us another picture of Omar,' Maryam interjected before Rubiah could begin again. Badgering the witness, that's what they called it on TV crime dramas from America, and that's clearly what Rubiah was doing. 'Everyone else we've spoken to about him whispers and looks over their shoulder, as if they expect to see him behind them with a pelesit on his shoulder.'

'He seems to cultivate it,' Deraman agreed. 'He's a gifted bomoh, I've said it before. I'm sure his jampi are very effective – that's why people still go to him even if they're a bit frightened.'

'Do you think he's as effective with black magic?' Maryam asked.

'I think he's effective,' he answered drily, 'in whatever magic.'

'Do you think he might have been responsible for the top flying up and hitting Che Hassan?' Rubiah continued. 'Could it happen?'

Deraman looked uncomfortable, not for the first time during this conversation. He sighed and lit another cigarette. 'Look,' he began slowly, 'I don't know what you want me to say. If you're asking me if I think Omar is a good enough bomoh to do that kind of magic, to make a top as heavy as a stone fly up for no reason and kill an innocent man just sitting there? I do.' He paused and grunted. 'I'll tell you there aren't many people in Kelantan I'd say that about. It's quite a feat. Would he do it?' He paused again. 'I don't know. If all the traces of the Omar I knew once upon a time are gone, then I guess he would. But I don't know that.'

He looked pained. 'I can't say,' he said, more loudly, with a hint of anger in his voice. 'You keep asking me questions I just can't answer, no matter how many times you put them to me. Alright? I think he could do it but I don't know, I really don't know, if he would.'

He shook his head and glared at Rubiah. 'Is that enough?'

'Yes, it is,' Maryam leapt into the fray, afraid Rubiah might ask him one more question and have him explode. 'You've been very helpful, Che Deraman, and we're very grateful for what you've told us. It's helped a lot.' She gave Rubiah a sharp look and began readying to leave.

'Thank you,' she said, sincerely. 'Please let us know if you think of anything else. We live in Kampong Penambang, just across the river, and we can come to talk to you anytime.' She quietly pushed Rubiah out ahead of her, though Rubiah just as quietly resisted. With a final smile and well-aimed shove, she got them out the door and down the steps and headed in the direction of the ferry.

Chapter XVIII

'Now you can see what not to do,' Maryam told Aliza when they were home again. 'You don't keep pursuing someone until they get angry. Unless of course you think they're guilty of a crime,' she allowed. 'We aren't accusing Che Deraman of anything, just wanting to get some background and maybe some…insights into our case. There isn't any point in pushing him.'

'I would never have thought of Omar like that,' Aliza considered. 'A regular guy who wasn't born to be quite so ugly. I thought his face represented his nature.'

'It might now,' Maryam warned her. 'His regular guy days are way behind him.'

Aliza sighed. 'Do you think his wife's illness drove him to it?'

'Unless he did it to her. Rubiah thinks he did.'

Aliza nodded. 'Maybe she's too convinced.'

Maryam put down the large spoon she was using to stir the vegetables for dinner. 'We've heard another perspective on Omar, yes, but it doesn't make what we thought before untrue,' she lectured Aliza. 'Don't make the mistake of jumping right to the opposite outlook and now decide Omar is really a nice, loving husband who's been badly misunderstood. He isn't that, even if we've heard about a glimmer of humanity from Che Deraman.

'Remember, he attacked me too during that whole kite flying case. I know that no matter how human someone makes him seem, he's still evil. Maybe not as evil as we thought,' she admitted, picking up her spoon again and stirring the pot. The green beans in coconut milk were ready for the serving bowl, and dinner was only moments away. 'But there's still plenty of room for him to be dangerous. Don't forget that. Think of Osman!'

'Rahman says he's getting better slowly,' Aliza said.

'Exactly,' Maryam agreed, handing her the beans and grilled fish to lay on the table. Maryam herself prepared the rice server. 'Slowly. He's lucky it wasn't worse. Don't think Omar isn't dangerous, because he is, and I don't want anything happening to you. Promise me,' she said suddenly. 'Promise me you won't go off by yourself looking for trouble with him.'

She gave Aliza a searching look, but she knew, even as she said it, it would be nearly impossible to keep Aliza away from this investigation. At least Rahman would look out for her.

***

The discussion had preyed on Deraman's mind, though he tried to escape it. He sat brooding on his porch at twilight, putting off his *Maghrib* prayers; not quite in a temper, but not really in a good mood either. His wife tried the most popular reaction first, that of ignoring him and hoping he pulled himself out of it, but it didn't seem to be working. Finally, she moved to Plan B: speaking to him directly. This course of action had its risks, as it might serve to further irritate him rather than calm him down, but something had to be done.

She sat down next to him on the porch, looking out into the fading light and the small bats beginning to leave their caves and fly among the trees.

'Dinner will be ready soon,' she offered her opening gambit.

He grunted without turning to look at her.

'Difficult conversation?' she asked. This was, she knew from experience, the make or break remark. Either he'd snap at her and refuse to speak, or it would let flow a torrent of words and she'd find out everything. She held her breath … it could go either way.

'You remember Omar, don't you?' he began. It was the second option, thank heaven. She relaxed against the wall and prepared to hear the whole story. It promised to be a good one. She nodded, answering him.

'We haven't seen him for ages,' he continued, still watching the bats. 'That's the way I wanted it. He was far too involved in these strange things, black magic, knowledge about things I don't want to know about. No one should know about. It made my skin crawl.

'And now these two ladies from Kampong Penambang come here asking about him. They've heard he's killed people with black magic. It's all over Kelantan that he does things like that.'

'Do you think it's true?'

'How do I know?' he answered crankily. 'I don't see him. I don't want to.' He went silent, and his wife waited patiently for his words to start again.

'I feel I'm going to have to see him again.'

'What?'

He nodded, finally looking at her. 'I know, but once he was my friend and he's going to end up killed if this continues. People are already afraid of him. They'll believe anything about him, and maybe they're right. Maybe he does kill people. But no one will leave him alone to continue killing if it goes on like this.

'Who else is there?' he asked rhetorically. 'No family, no friends anymore. No one but his pelesit, that is, if he actually has one. What a mess,' he ended sadly.

'Does it have to be you, Man?' his wife asked anxiously. 'I mean, it really could be dangerous! Why *korek lubang ulat*, dig up worms and ask for trouble?'

'You think I should leave it alone?' he asked softly.

'Yes!' she agreed heartily. 'You should. You don't know him anymore and he could be everything people say. Or worse!'

'I have to try,' he said simply, rising to his feet to go inside.

'Then I'm coming with you,' she said firmly. 'Don't even think about telling me not to.'

He smiled and shook his head, acknowledging he could not fight it, then walked into the house to complete his prayers before dinner.

***

Osman and his men made a trip to the border with Thailand at Rantau Panjang, to see the lay of the land where they were supposedly encouraging the trade in questionable and morally degenerate movies. It looked pretty much as Osman expected:

a modern bridge with immigration and customs on either side, manned by uniformed officers. And below it, a large, shallow muddy river meandering slowly, with steep, eroded banks, now rocky and denuded of any plant growth. These banks constituted the real entry into either Malaysia or Thailand so the customs huts on the bridge could be kept in all their pristine glory. Men scuttled up and down the banks carrying large sacks of Thai Jasmine rice bound for the markets of Kota Bharu, often stopping half a mile or so down the tracks to throw the sacks of rice into the trains once they were out of sight of officials of either country. It was not going on now, as the Kota Bharu police stood there in the middle of the day; the trade was conducted primarily in the twilight or at night, when it wasn't quite so obvious.

'This is where the movies come in?' Osman asked, surveying the scene and the commercial activity between the markets in Rantau Panjang on the Kelantan side and Sungei Golok on the Thai side. It seemed pretty lively and apparently legal.

'Well, Sungei Golok is known for its nightlife,' one of his men explained. 'You know, drinking, women, gambling, that sort of thing.'

'Movies?'

The man shrugged fatalistically. 'This is where they'd come from. It's kind of the only place.' His colleagues nodded solemnly.

'And I allow it?' Osman asked, shocked that anyone would believe he held sway over all this.

'I don't see how we have much to do with it,' another policeman said doubtfully. 'That would be the border police.'

'I think you need to be seen here,' Rahman took the

conversation back to the practical. 'People need to remember they saw you here when the talk is that you stopped it all. Look unhappy about it.'

Osman obediently wrinkled his brow and frowned at the river, crossing his arms and giving as good a performance of a stern taskmaster as he was capable. His team did the same, looking much like a group of sheriffs swaggering into a lawless western Cowtown.

After a few minutes, Rahman deemed they were done. They'd been very visible; they'd looked very disapproving. Now it was time for their showdown in a Rantau Panjang coffee house, where Ah Pak was delivering his friend for a public scolding. They walked in a group down the streets of the town, scowling at anyone who'd meet their eyes, invading the arranged coffee shop and arranging themselves around the two Chinese merchants waiting for them.

Ah Pak ordered coffees all around; it was very hot, after all, and there was no point staging a dressing down while thirsty. His friend, the appointed villain, tried to look frightened, or at least nervous, but in fact remained fairly phlegmatic and even philosophical, as if being censured by the police was one of the costs of doing business.

Introductions were made, and Osman looked daggers at Ah Pak's friend, and then at Ah Pak too, for good measure. He explained loudly that any importation of salacious materials would stop immediately, right now, and never resume. If he ever found out it started again, there'd be jail time at the very least, not to mention earning the undying enmity of the Kota Bharu, and very possibly the Rantau Panjang, police force, who would make it their job to make his life miserable.

Ah Pak and his friend hung their heads and vowed never to do anything like this again. Osman gave them a final glare, and then everyone began drinking their coffee and exchanging gossip. The owner of the coffee shop did not wait more than five minutes after they all left to tell everyone hanging around the main market what had transpired, and to marvel at the toughness and probity of the Kota Bharu police. Ah Pak had done very well indeed.

***

Deraman and his wife, Anim, took their motorbike across the bridge to Kota Bharu, and then through Kampong Penambang towards the beach. Anim sat decorously side-saddle behind him, he drove with a headcloth to hold back his hair. He was nervous, reluctant to arrive, hoping that maybe Omar would be out, gone, moved away, and he would therefore have done the right thing without having to confront him. It was childish, he admitted to himself, and most unlikely. Having come this far, he would do what he set out to do, even though it might be awkward.

At Cabang Tiga, he turned into the kampong, to the house he remembered from so many years ago. He hadn't been there in, well, he didn't know how long. Since he was a friend of Omar's. Since they were young men together with similar interests, both at the beginning of their adult lives: newly married, babies on the way, at least for Deraman. He felt as though the short ride into the village was a trip through time rather than space, moving into his past instead of just through Cabang Tiga. Anim sensed his anxiety, and became anxious herself, but congratulated herself on doing the right thing in going with him for support.

Deraman slowly parked the motorbike and looked up at the ladder to Omar's house as if it were Mount Everest, and he wondered how he'd ever make it. Omar, hearing the noise, came to the door of his house and stood on the porch, a wide smile coming into being piece by piece. Deraman thought he could see each separate muscle at work creating the expression.

'Deraman!'

Deraman smiled sheepishly. 'It's me, yes.'

Omar peered into the darkness. 'Is that Cik Anim with you? Really?'

Anim smiled at him, far more spiritedly than she'd meant to, and nodded.

'You've come to visit! What an occasion! Come up, come up,' he said enthusiastically. He ushered them up to the porch and ducked into the house to bring out some kerosene lanterns. He laughed as he put them out. 'Not what you're used to, I'm sure, it's all very basic here. Not like Kampong Laut, right? You must have such a busy house with children and—are there grandchildren yet? I thought so! How nice for you! Well, we're certainly glad to see you here, aren't we, Jah?' He turned to his wife, who glided unconsciously onto the porch, her eyes staring off into nothing, her expression carved from stone. Without a word she went to the corner of the porch and sat facing out into the night, her back to her guests and her husband, a silent watcher. Deraman immediately understood why Rubiah had described her as a zombie, and he felt fleeting shame he had smacked her down when she said it. She had been quite accurate.

'Ah, Jah isn't feeling quite herself this evening,' Omar explained smoothly. 'She's so pleased to see you, I know, but she's been...a bit unwell lately.'

'We've known each other a long time,' Deraman began, angry at himself for beginning with such a cliché. Surely there were more dynamic ways to open a conversation. He cleared his throat to redeem his rhetoric. 'You don't need to apologize to us, Omar. We're very old friends. I remember when Cik Jah began to suffer her...illness, yes. It doesn't seem to have improved.'

Omar's smile faltered. 'No, I can't say it has, though of course, we always have faith that it might, at any time. Sometimes she's better, but lately it hasn't been too good. I mean,' he amended, 'she's healthy but for her mind. She isn't there so much of the time,' he finished slowly, looking more depressed. 'I don't know where her mind goes, she never tells me.'

'Does she speak often?' Deraman probed.

'Not too often. Sometimes though, she comes right out of it and I think, maybe this is the time where she throws off this curtain, these bars which are holding her! And then, after a few minutes, she slows down again, like a car running out of gas and falls back into this silence.'

They sat in their own silence, thinking about what he'd said. Deraman cleared his throat again. 'Have you tried...?'

'What haven't I tried? Bomoh, hospitals, medicine, *main puteri*. I can't tell myself whether she's possessed by a spirit, or just losing her semangat, her energy. If it is a spirit, though, it isn't saying anything. I don't know what it wants.' He looked frightened for a moment, or perhaps it was a trick of the flickering lantern. 'Spirits, you know, they usually take over because they want something. What would be the use of a spirit possessing her and not saying a word about what it wants? How does it expect me to find out and provide it if it won't say anything? Right?'

Deraman agreed. Anim had moved over to sit next to Jah and stroke her arm, trying to get through to her somehow that friends were here and could help her. Jah didn't react at all, she might have been inanimate. Anim was tempted to bend her head to Jah's shoulder and weep but feared the anxiety she felt being here might have overwhelmed her and made her more emotional than was really healthy. She was usually the steadiest of women, difficult to upset, Apollonian in her emotions. And here she was getting ready to cry all over this already suffering woman, making things worse than they already were.

Anim looked around, watching Deraman and Omar speaking softly together, only partially lit by the small yellow flame. It was no doubt the night and the unsteady light, but it seemed to her that Omar was looking at her more than at Deraman, and that it was Anim who interested him, not the silent and immobile Jah. Anim began to fear; but fear what, she wasn't sure. It was as if, she tried to articulate to herself, and later to Deraman, that Omar wanted to take her life, her consciousness, her energy, and pass it into Jah, leaving Anim a carved case from which all those thoughts which made her herself would have been leached, given to someone else.

She tamped down the panic which began to rise in her. How

crazy would she look to leap to her feet and pull her husband off the porch, spewing nonsense about her semangat being stolen, her self extinguished. And all this would be in the context of what? Sitting on the porch, with Omar not even speaking to her? People would be right to fear for her reason, as she herself was now beginning to do. Her breathing became faster as she felt she could not get enough oxygen into her lungs, and soon she was audibly gasping for breath. She felt dizzy, disoriented, clumsy. Her limbs did not obey her, her hands scrabbled against the wooden boards, and suddenly, Jah turned to look at her. Jah was waking up as she was falling into a dark pit.

Any thoughts of embarrassment fled from her mind; she panicked. If she didn't leave now, she'd never leave, not as Anim at any rate. And Jah would live off her like a vampire who didn't need blood, only life. She cried out as loudly as she could. She felt she was shrieking, but Deraman heard only the smallest of sighs, and turned to see his wife lying on the floor, her hands reaching out to him but grasping only the wooden floor, her eyes emptying of light.

He leapt to his feet and pulled her up against him. 'Anim,' he cried loudly. 'Listen to me!' She tried to nod to show him she was, and she clutched his shoulders as though she would never let go. She tried to speak but could not. Jah stood up behind her.

'It's such a shame, after not seeing her for so long, she seems to be ill,' Jah said, patting Anim on the back and smiling at Deraman. 'Perhaps some tea?' She smiled at Omar as well and walked into the house to prepare refreshments. Omar smiled broadly at her.

'See? I told you! Sometimes she comes out of it.'

Deraman was already dragging Anim down the ladder to the bike. 'You're leaving?' Omar asked with concern. 'No! Not when Jah has just rejoined us. You must stay!'

Deraman could not even answer. He placed Anim on the back of the bike and took her face in both her hands. 'Listen to me,' he said urgently. 'Can you hold on to me? Can you make it? Pay attention!'

She seemed to sway a little but stiffened her back and nodded. She wanted to leave as badly as she'd ever wanted anything in her life. She'd die if she stayed here even a few minutes more. Deraman got on the bike and she hugged him around the waist, even though that was shocking behaviour for a respectable wife and mother, who was supposed to balance by holding on to the back of the seat. But she'd fall over if she did that, and anyway, this was an emergency. And it was dark, Alhamdulillah, so no one would see.

Deraman wanted to roar out of the village and onto the main road, perhaps leaving skid marks as he turned off the dirt onto the asphalt. But he could not, not without possibly leaving Anim in the street, so he drove slowly home, feeling her gain strength with every mile farther from Omar's house.

Chapter XIX

'So, that's what I think he does,' Deraman concluded, leaning back against the cushions on Maryam's living room couch. His audience was silent, spellbound, willing him to tell them more.

'I apologize to you, Kakak Rubiah,' he said, squaring his shoulders and stepping up to admit he was wrong. 'You were right. It is just like those Indonesian zombie movies.' That was a sentence he never thought he'd utter, but honour demanded he acknowledge his mistakes.

'It's nothing,' Rubiah assured him, but she could not camouflage her pride in calling this correctly. She modestly dipped her head so she wouldn't look as though she was preening.

'Wait,' Mamat urged, thinking hard. 'You think, this is what you're saying: Omar has the power to take the semangat from someone, to suck it out of them, and pour it into his wife to bring her back to life for a little while.'

Deraman nodded sadly. It was not a happy thing to say.

'Are there a lot of people walking around who've been turned into zombies themselves?' Mamat pursued, disbelieving. At this rate, most of Kelantan could be sitting motionless and empty. Like pod people: he'd seen *The Invasion of the Body Snatchers* years before, but he hadn't foreseen he'd be discussing it as though it were actual history. The world had taken a very strange turn.

Deraman sighed, putting a world of sorrow into it. 'I don't think so,' he said, considering. 'Look at my wife,' he waved a hand in her direction where she sat between Maryam and Rubiah. 'She's alright now. I think Che Osman will be alright as well. It's temporary, I believe. Although,' he drifted off, his eyes focused on the far wall, 'these are both people we rescued before the draining was finished, so to speak.' His audience shuddered. 'I don't know what might have happened if he'd had enough time to keep going. Would the other person die? I don't know. Maybe,' he paused, shifting his eyes back to the here and now and looking at Rahman, 'it would be interesting to ask around Cabang Tiga and see if there were people who seemed to be possessed and then recovered. See if he's using people to bring Cik Jah back even for a little while.'

Aliza exchanged a look with Rahman. Would that really be a line of inquiry for the police? Rahman might be considered crazy for asking, or he might just scare the daylights out of his officers. After all, there was already buzz about Osman's indisposition, which no one believed was simply exhaustion from overwork, as Azrina had explained. Though the officers who'd accompanied Rahman on the rescue were sworn to secrecy, these things had a way of leaking out even with the best of intentions. A flock of people who'd had the same thing could be terrifying to the populace, and Rahman wasn't sure it wouldn't turn violent. If he found his family had been hurt, or feared they would be, well, you could hardly blame people for getting worked up.

'Was it a pelesit?' Aliza asked. 'Or just a jampi?'

'I didn't see a pelesit,' Anim answered. She insisted she was fine but admitted to herself she was still jumpy. There was still a part of her she wasn't sure had quite come back, but she was determined to ignore it. 'Of course, it was at night and it could be very small.'

'Or invisible,' Rubiah interjected.

'That too, so I could have missed it. It came on so suddenly. It was as though a plug had been pulled all of a sudden.'

Maryam patted her knee and smiled at her. 'You've been really brave,' she told Anim. 'Not many people would be able to come back from such a fright.'

Maryam was one of those people who had – just a couple years ago, was it? She'd had an experience as a were-tiger, or maybe it was the delusion of being a were-tiger, but it was so real. Maryam was not sure she'd ever recover her life, or whether she'd spend the rest of her life in that shadow world as a tiger spirit. It had a been a very difficult recuperation, and one which her family did not care to discuss. She believed it might be the same for Anim and resolved to try to talk to her and invite her to share the burden. There were so few people who could really empathize with what had happened to her.

'I felt,' Anim struggled to explain, 'I felt…like I was being pulled out to sea, where I couldn't fight and I could feel my life leaving me, leaking out of me…' She became silent, despairing of ever being able to describe the whoosh of her soul, her energy, her very being just leaving her.

'And you were…?'

'Empty,' she said, almost whispering. 'I wasn't anything anymore. I guess that's what it's like when you die. You're just... gone. Do you think so?'

'How can we know?' Maryam answered practically. 'But more important, how are you now? What do you feel like now?'

Anim brushed some non-existent hair off her forehead. 'Better, I guess. I mean I'm here, aren't I? Talking and making sense. I feel like a person. What I mean is,' she struggled and thought about exactly what she meant to say, 'I'm not empty anymore. But also, I'm not really totally me, either. It's kind of frightening.'

'It's going to take time,' Maryam assured her kindly. 'A long time. But in the meantime, it's best, that is, I think it is, to act as though you're over it. Because, and I'm telling you this from my own experience, if you don't, your family will be terrified, and people will start to avoid you. I know it isn't fair,' Maryam said sympathetically, 'and maybe you feel you'd like to talk about it, but at least my family couldn't bear it. Only Cik Rubiah, and thank God for her, would talk to me about it but even she didn't want to after a while. It frightens people, you know. It's like you're a messenger from another world, a bad one.'

Anim nodded, silent.

'I won't be afraid,' Maryam assured her. 'I know just what it's like, so I won't think you're crazy.' She smiled. 'It's strange how sometimes the people you're closest to just can't do anything for you.' She redirected her attention to Deraman and the others, who were deep in conversation.

'Who knows what he's doing?' she heard Deraman say to Rubiah. 'Maybe all this talk about his jampi and black magic and all that,' he finished lamely, not willing to use more pithy expressions around such respected Mak Cik and aspiring detectives such as Aliza. 'Maybe he's getting deeper into this to try to bring his wife back.'

'Maybe he's the one who put her there in the first place,' Rubiah replied curtly. 'Isn't that possible? What kind of disease does she have that makes her like that? I mean, I know older people who begin to forget things, of course, and they can be vague and or confused. But they don't turn to stone like she did. You laughed at me before,' she drew herself up to defend her thesis, 'but I think I was on the right track. She's a zombie and he made her that way. Now he's guilty and trying to undo it, but it might be too late, and besides, he needs to drain other people to try to make her human again.'

She looked sharply at Mamat and Rahman, and to her own husband as well, daring them to brush off her thoughts again. They'd tried to do it before and they were wrong, so now, of course, they accepted it. Mamat looked to Deraman for direction, and he in turn was staring at his wife.

'What do you think?' he asked her quietly. 'You were the most affected by it. Do you think he made her what she is?'

Anim thought about it, looking inward, silent for longer than anyone thought was comfortable. 'I do. I think he's so guilty, he'd do anything to make her better. He doesn't care about anyone else. That's why he's always experimenting. If his experiments hurt other people, or even kill them, I don't think he counts that as being important. If only he can undo what he's done to her, he thinks he can make everything right again.

'Of course, each person he touches, each life he ruins, makes it less likely he can bring her back. The evil is piling up, you see. He knows it, and it makes him frantic. He's very dangerous now, more than ever.'

She looked up and took a deep, sudden breath, as if she'd just woken up and looked around wide-eyed. 'What did I say?' she asked.

They stared at her in wonder. 'You, you don't know?' her husband asked. 'Where did it come from?'

She shook her head. 'Tell me. What did I say?'

Chapter XX

'That was horrifying,' Aliza whispered to Rahman as they walked through now-sleeping Kampong Penambang. 'I don't know what to think.'

'I think we're getting very far away from Hassan's death, that's what I think. That's how this started, isn't it? And now we're in the middle of the living dead. I don't like it.'

'Of course not! Who likes it? But it seems everywhere we turn there's Omar. Lurking.'

'Or we could say everywhere we turn we see Omar because that's what we're expecting, right?'

Aliza was silent. 'I think it's time to just find out what happened to kill Hassan, and then close this investigation. We're all on the way to becoming zombies,' Rahman added morosely. 'Look at what's happened: that guy your mother spoke to falls from the stairs in his house and dies, Hassan dies at a top-spinning contest, Osman gets, I don't know what you call it, zombified. Now Cik Anim.' He spluttered in frustration. 'What happens next?' he demanded, but of course, Aliza didn't know.

'And with all this, we still don't know…'

'I think we might,' Aliza interrupted him. 'I think we're all thinking about it but we aren't saying it,' she continued, purposely looking ahead and not at him so she could in all conscience keep talking without receiving any meaningful looks. 'I think Omar was experimenting again with his jampi and ended up letting the top fly after it hit. I think we all believe that,' she continued bravely.

'I don't, not really,' Rahman muttered.

She ignored him. 'So, to me the question is how did he do it? How did he get to Ramli, who I think had no idea it was happening. I think Ramli's innocent,' she declared.

'You've been thinking about this a lot,' Rahman commented.

'I have,' she agreed. 'How did he get to Ramli? Ramli doesn't use him. No one saw him at the contest. Did he have someone who slipped in his magic? Or,' she paused, thinking hard, 'It could be Deraman.'

'What? No. He wouldn't go along with that.'

'No, not if he knew. But if he were duped…If he didn't know and Omar slipped something into his stuff so Deraman didn't know it and inadvertently gave it to Ramli and then it caused the top…'

'Hold on,' Rahman said as they reached their house. 'Deraman said he hadn't seen Omar in years. How would that happen?'

Aliza shook her head. 'I know, that's the problem. I just can't figure out how it happened yet. Or to understand why he would want to kill Hassan.'

'It's a big problem. You can't even show how Omar got any magic to the contest. Don't say pelesit,' he cautioned her. 'I can't stand hearing about it.'

'I wasn't going to. But I just know Omar was involved in it.'

Rahman shook his head sadly. The more he knew, the less he knew.

***

'Mak, it's like this. Omar knew Hassan, and Omar knew Deraman. Deraman gave his jampi to Ramli, and Ramli's top killed Hassan. It's all related. Can't you see?'

'I can,' Maryam assured her, 'but I still can't see how Omar managed to affect this contest. After all Deraman has said, I don't imagine he'd take anything from Omar and pass it on, do you? No, it would have to be something else,' she said, almost to herself.

She turned to pick Yunus off the floor before he headed toward the hot stove. 'Look how quickly he scoots around already,' she wondered to Aliza. 'He's way ahead of himself.'

'He'll have to be, if he's going to survive his sister,' Aliza informed her. 'Zakaria had better catch up soon, poor thing, or else he'll soon find…'

'What?' Ashikin asked as she came through the yard to the kitchen. 'What will Zakaria find?'

'Nuraini will be all over him.'

'That,' she said flatly, making herself comfortable on the steps. 'Mak, how has he been?'

'Wonderful. Such a good baby,' Maryam told her. Yunus crowed as though agreeing with her assessment.

'You're right about Nuraini,' Ashikin continued. 'She's at

least trying to look like she cares about them, but I don't buy it.' She examined her nails with a frown. 'I'm at my wits' end with her. I just don't know what to do. Daud says we need to be stricter with her, but I'm afraid she'll just pretend and as soon as our backs are turned she'll make their lives miserable.'

'You don't really think that!' Maryam cried. 'This is Nuraini we're talking about. Quite the little princess I agree, but actually being mean, well, I don't agree.'

'I do,' Aliza interjected.

'You're cynical,' her mother told her, and then proceeded to ignore her. 'Kin, you're losing perspective on her. She's just a little girl who's a little jealous, that's all.'

Ashikin said nothing but raised her eyebrows to signify doubt and shared a look with Aliza which clearly advised her they would talk later, when they could be perfectly frank with each other. Maryam caught the look but chose to ignore it, loathe to be trapped in another conversation about Nuraini's behaviour. Strangely, when speaking to Mamat, who refused to see anything wrong in her, she took the position that Nuraini needed to be disciplined, but with Ashikin, who took a more hard-headed approach, she counselled patience and defended her grandchild. She wondered briefly if this dynamic explained Mamat's attitude when faced with a disapproving family. Perhaps he too felt he had to defend Nuraini from those inclined to punish her.

'How's your case coming?' Ashikin interrupted her thoughts.

Maryam shook her head. 'I don't know,' she admitted, with a quick look at Aliza. 'It started out simply: did Ramli throw the top to kill Hassan or not? A straightforward question which deserves a straightforward answer. But now it's become tangled in black magic and zombies...'

'Zombies?' Ashikin asked incredulously.

Maryam nodded. 'I know. Can you imagine? Zombies. And whether Omar was involved...'

'Of course he was,' Aliza snorted.

'And what kind of magic he used,' Maryam finished. 'It's anything but straightforward now. It gives me a headache.'

'Mak Cik Rubiah's solved it already,' Ashikin commented. 'It's that bomoh.'

'Omar,' Aliza supplied the name.

'Him,' Ashikin agreed. 'He and his pelesit are all over Kelantan.'

'She might be right,' Aliza said. 'Nothing would surprise me anymore.'

'Perhaps you've wandered a bit far from the case,' Ashikin suggested delicately. 'Maybe it's time to get back to what actually happened and work with it. You know. Just stick to how that guy was killed and that's all.'

'That's what I'm trying to do', Maryam answered, annoyed. 'Do you think I want to wander around talking about black magic and zombies? No! And then Osman's been hurt...'

'He's half a zombie,' Aliza explained helpfully. 'Rahman saved him right before he went under.'

'Aren't you worried about this bomoh turning all of us into zombies?'

'You've seen too many movies,' Maryam informed her crisply, although she didn't feel nearly as sure as she sounded.

She'd believed Omar was dangerous before, but now she felt he was not only dangerous, but at least half mad.

Still, she laid out everything you she knew about the case for Ashikin, who had an uncanny knack for coming to the heart of a problem when other people couldn't find it. Aliza prompted her when she gave any detail insufficient emphasis and editorialized where she felt she had a theory. Both Maryam and Aliza leaned back when they were finished to hear Ashikin's analysis.

'Well,' Ashikin began, after a long silence punctuated by elegant sips of coffee, 'it's a mess. I don't think Ramli killed Hassan on purpose and neither do you, so let's stop pretending that's still on the table. From Ramli's perspective, a terrible accident. No doubt he feels guilty, I know I would. But still, he wasn't trying to do it, and if he'd tried, he'd never have managed it. And no one would be stupid enough to do something like that in front of all those people if he meant for it to happen.

'No,' Ashikin concluded, 'Ramli's an unfortunate accidental killer. Maybe not even a killer. Anyway, if that's all there is, you might as well go talk to Osman and tell him Ramli's innocent.'

She lit a cigarette passed to her by her mother, who also lit one. Maryam gave Aliza a long look and did not offer her any; clearly, she was married but hadn't yet achieved smoking status. Aliza tried to ignore it, but it bothered her just the same.

'So, the question that everyone wants to know the answer to is: who's responsible? Someone is, this was no accident of nature. No, this was manmade.' Ashikin tipped her face up toward the roof and blew smoke at it. 'Omar seems likely. He's crazy, he's mean, he's always trying strange magic to do all kinds of evil things. He could well have done it, though how it would help his wife I can't imagine. I'm lucky that I can't think like he does. What a life it must be inside his head.' She shuddered.

'Do you think he did it?'

'I don't know.' Maryam's shoulders slumped and she realized how much she'd hoped that Ashikin would straighten it all out for her in a moment. 'But it's a bomoh, I feel sure of that.'

'What does that mean? Are we to start calling on every bomoh in Kelantan? It has to be someone who knows the people involved, not just…'

'I know that,' Ashikin answered with irritation. 'I'm just saying. It has to be someone with powerful magic to make this happen. It isn't going to be just anyone. Concentrate on that.'

'That's what I'm doing!' Maryam cried in exasperation.

'Then you're halfway there.'

Chapter XXI

Omar sat quietly on the small porch of his house, half-heartedly drinking coffee and thinking about how his life had worked out. His wife sat beside him, inert; her recent return to him had lasted a full day and made him so happy he nearly dissolved into tears. But then, as always, she slipped away and became the lifeless effigy she'd turned into.

Jah had been his life. He'd fallen in love with her the first time he'd seen her – it was a cliché, he knew, but in his case it was true. He'd been a young bomoh-in-training, following his teacher to a job in Semut Api, the village right on the coast down the road from his home in Cabang Tiga. As they scuffed through the sand between the houses, Omar saw a young woman herding the family's goats into a small enclosure for the evening. She turned and looked at him, gave him the smallest possible smile, and returned to her attention to her recalcitrant animals. Omar could not forget that smile.

He returned two days later, at the same time, hoping to find her with the goats again. She wasn't there, and the animals were scattered around the kampong regarding him with the peculiarly baleful gaze that is a specialty of the species. He nearly asked one of them where she was, before controlling his eagerness and calming down. He didn't see anyone around. It was late afternoon and the fishing boats were returning; most of the village was down at the beach to meet them and sell the day's catch. Feeling himself in a deserted landscape, he milled around aimlessly following the goats, when suddenly, an older man appeared. Whether he'd been resting in his house or returning from the beach Omar had no idea, but he tried valiantly to look like he had something useful to do.

He did not impress the man. 'What are you doing?' he asked Omar, looking puzzled. 'Are you…tracking the goats?' He might as well have asked if Omar were dim-witted or just looked like it.

'No,' Omar assured him, having lost all sense of dignity, 'I'm not following goats.'

'It looks like you are.'

'Maybe it does,' he admitted, 'but I'm not.'

The man crossed his arms and waited to see what excuse Omar would dredge up.

'I'm looking for someone.'

'A goat?'

'Forget the goats. No, I'm looking for a girl I saw here a couple of days ago.'

The man's eyebrows rose. 'This is what you call looking for her?'

'I didn't see anyone here, so I'm kind of…waiting to see if she comes back so I can meet her.'

The man stood silent.

'I don't really know her,' Omar continued, feeling himself

losing ground with every word. If he could have ordered the sand to open up and swallow him, he would have gladly done so. 'I saw her the day before yesterday, when I was here to work with Pak Amin, the bomoh. I thought maybe I'd come by and introduce myself...'

'Where did you see her?'

'Here! She was bringing the goats in and so I thought she'd be here again today.' Omar could not meet the man's eyes. 'It's probably time I went, I guess she won't be here today.' He began backing away, praying he wouldn't trip over a goat and complete his humiliation.

The man followed him with his eyes and said nothing. As Omar walked away from the house, back towards the road, he saw her. There she was, carrying a small package from the store. He was flooded with relief.

He beamed at her. She looked at him both pleased and wary and smiled back.

'Good evening,' he began, with overflowing enthusiasm. 'I don't know if you remember me, I was here the day before...'

'I remember you,' she said simply.

He could not even turn down his smile, although he tried. 'I thought I'd come back and introduce myself,' he said politely.

She turned to the man who was now walking up to them. 'Ayah', she said, 'this is...'

'Omar,' he added.

The man looked unimpressed. 'This is the girl you were looking for?' he asked.

Omar nodded. The man sighed. 'He saw you the day before

yesterday,' he told his daughter, 'and I saw him today walking around with the goats looking for you. I guess he thought they'd know where you were.'

She burst into peals of laughter, and Omar smiled as well. Somehow his idiocy now seemed possibly charming rather than hopeless, and at any rate, he'd found her.

Jah's father never tired of telling the story of how he'd met Omar, embellishing it to the point where his listeners could be forgiven for thinking that Omar had been discovered actually speaking to the goats and getting answers from them. But from this unpromising start, he'd married Jah and never seriously looked at another woman since.

They'd been heartbroken when they realized they'd never have children. They were planning to adopt a child, or two, and then Jah began having 'spells' where she seemed to wander away from her body. It was at this time that Omar's study of magic took a turn into a more serious, and unapproved area. He would try anything to keep Jah from slipping away from him and used the bomoh's arts to keep her energy 'in,' and if necessary, to bring other energy into her.

It had become more difficult through the years, as her spells increased in length and severity. Whereas in the beginning she was forgetful and flustered, as the years went on, she became wooden, silent, no longer present. Days would go by with no word from her, nor with any voluntary motion.

Omar's interest in sports and the magic that went with it grew out of his personal dilemma. Who better than athletes to have a surfeit of energy brought to the highest peak possible? And what better use for that energy than to reanimate Jah? Not, Omar assured himself, that he would use every athlete for such purposes. No indeed, for the most part he experimented with different jampi to improve performance, and to see how far he could take his power. This occasionally had the consequence of injuring the athlete, but Omar believed in the pursuit of science, there were bound to be mistakes: they were a learning opportunity.

For people who got in his way, or irritated him, or appeared to threaten the most important project in his life, Omar was unforgiving. He had little use for Maryam, Rubiah and their ilk, who would pry into his business, investigating things he did not personally consider important. And if they impinged on his freedom to work, and placed Jah in possible danger, then he would not hesitate in doing his best to swat them to the side and get them out of the way. It wasn't done with anger or malice, Omar would have explained. It was just necessary.

Chapter XXII

Ramli couldn't sleep, wouldn't sleep. Immediately after the accident he felt sorry, of course he did, for Hassan. Certainly he had no intention of killing the man – it had not even crossed his mind. He was shocked to see him die while innocently watching the contest. He was even more shocked to realize he had held the murder weapon himself, although with no thought at all to use it in such a perversion of its actual purpose. But he could not work himself into actual guilt, because he never wanted to do it. As far as agency went, this had nothing to do with him.

And yet, he was there. He'd held the top and thrown it as hard as he could. He never aimed at anything save the ground, and he did not assign to himself the ability to make tops fly. It could only be the work of someone else, someone knowledgeable in these arts, someone for whom murder was an interesting hobby, nothing more.

After the first shock had faded, he found himself pursued by regret and contrition. Though even as he contemplated his feelings he could not recognize himself as a murderer, and when he thought back on what he might have done to avoid it, he could actually come up with nothing more helpful than to never have taken up top spinning in the first place.

But wasn't only top spinning which provided such danger. People could, and did, find themselves garrotted by kite strings, or trampled by bulls, or poisoned or shot or drowned. Top spinning in and of itself did not prepare one for death. Still, Ramli could not shake the belief that he was somehow to blame; it was his fate which brought him to that particular field at that particular time to act as the instrument of Hassan's death. And this conviction would not let him rest.

Keriah noticed he seemed to be losing weight and was no longer willing to participate in the sport he loved. She put it down to an acute sensitivity and a reluctance to put himself in a position to harm anyone. But as time went by, she became concerned that his guilt was now far out of what she considered proportion to his role in this tragedy. It wasn't his fault, and as Keriah explained it, he was a victim here himself, used as a pawn by whoever had engineered this crime, and who had used the black arts (how else could it have happened?) to carry it through.

Her theory was fine as far as it went, and might even have been true, but Ramli did not seem to really believe it. Whenever she pressed it on him, he agreed with her, it explained it all and how could anyone accuse him of malice when he had absolutely none? Still, as he reminded himself at least once every hour, it was his hand which had held the top and his arm which had thrown it. Didn't that somehow make him complicit in the crime?

And while this ate away at his mind, it seemed also to eat away at his body, and this alarmed Keriah. She was familiar, as was everyone in Kelantan, with stories of how random people began to waste away, with no discernible reason for it, until they finally passed away, shrunken skeletons of their former selves. This was not a fate she wanted for her own family, and she suspected that whoever actually killed Hassan was now trying kill her husband. Moreover, she had a good idea of who that might be, for Omar's reputation preceded him, and one look at his grasshopper-like body made it clear he was evil. Good people, normal people as Keriah understood them, did not look like ambulatory corpses.

She brought her fears to Deraman, whom she knew and trusted as a good man and a clever bomoh, who could protect Ramli and keep Omar and his darkness away from them. She went to his house full of determination and anxious to get her plan implemented as quickly as it could be done.

She was greeted at the door by Anim, who called her husband in to consult with Keriah, while she sat nearby, filled with curiosity about this further development.

'It's Ramli,' Keriah began, running her finger around the saucer of her teacup, looking down at it while she thought. 'He's getting thin, you see, and I'm afraid he's falling ill from guilt in all this, though it isn't his fault at all. The person whose fault it is should take the punishment, not Ramli, who never meant to hurt anyone. This is strong magic,' she explained forcefully, 'only a strong bomoh could do it. And only an evil one would,' she finished briskly. 'We all know it's that Omar. But everyone's afraid of him. I'm not that brave either, and if it weren't my husband at risk, I'd stay away from the whole situation. But I can't, because I'm afraid he's going to kill Ramli too, and then where will we all be?' She was surprised by her own tears rising as she spoke.

She'd had no idea she was so close to crying and wondered why she was.

'You have to help me,' she ended quickly. 'You have to save Ramli.'

Deraman looked concerned, which frightened her. Whenever she'd consulted him, he always seemed calm and competent and confident, which in turn calmed her down. But today he seemed none of those things, and she became more anxious just looking at him.

He answered slowly. 'I can try. And I will,' he assured her. 'But I must say, he's stronger than I thought he was. He's more evil, too. He's a real adversary. Not like some of the spirits I deal with. I know I'm stronger than they are, and they only need to be told, to be given a firm command. It's not like that with him,' he added almost to himself. 'He's the source. I don't know what he's done to himself to make them this way.'

'But you'll help,' she added, not as strongly as she had hoped to say it.

'I will,' he said simply. 'I can't let him do this to Ramli. I won't allow it.'

Keriah felt better hearing him announce it, though she wished he'd sounded more convinced. 'What do I need to do?' she asked.

He sighed. 'I've got to talk to Ramli first before I say anything. Meet me back at your house.'

***

Meanwhile, back at Kampong Penambang, Maryam wrestled

with the nature of guilt and innocence. Clearly, she thought, Ramli bore no guilt for the crime. She believed he never meant to hurt anyone, far less kill someone. Besides, she thought practically, if he'd wanted to kill someone, surely he could have found a more private place to do so than in front of a crowd of people who could act as witnesses. Maryam had seen from experience that often those who murdered other people were not necessarily brilliant, but even to that standard this would have been noteworthy.

If not Ramli, then who? Omar of course. Who else would conduct such a cold-blooded experiment in the strength of jampi? She still thought he'd killed Salleh and had so far gotten away with it, but this time, she thought grimly, he wouldn't escape justice. What was the police force she was thinking of? A TV program Yi used to watch when he was smaller. Sled dogs, snow… the *Mounties*. She, like them, always got her man, she thought proudly. It might have been a nice touch to have the red uniform as well, but Kota Bharu was probably far too hot to carry that off.

When she presented her results to Rubiah, she was greeted with an impatient snort. 'I told you at the start,' she said curtly, letting her cigarette hang out of the corner of her mouth, gangster-style. It was funny how they were beginning to adopt the mannerisms of detectives after several cases: Rubiah going for a Humphrey Bogart/Sam Spade gumshoe without the pistol, Maryam feeling a close kinship with the Royal Canadian Mounted Police. What next? she wondered. Perhaps detecting was beginning to get to them.

'I knew it was him.'

'You were right.'

'What brought you to this conclusion, finally?' Rubiah asked.

'It can't be Ramli. I don't see any reason for it.'

Rubiah nodded sagely. 'I know.'

'If not him, who would be controlling things behind the scenes? Omar. He doesn't care how many people he hurts.'

'True.'

'We'll need to talk to Osman about this. Or Rahman. I don't know how Osman is feeling, I've heard he isn't back at work yet.'

'We should go over and bring some cake to cheer him up. It would be rude not to stop by to see him.'

It was agreed they must.

Chapter XXIII

Osman was not back at work, he was barely back to the living room of his home. When Maryam and Rubiah appeared, bearing enormous quantities of Kelantan cakes and two papayas for a balanced diet, he was lying where he had been since he'd been rescued from Omar's house. He was roused from his bed by Azrina, who was delighted to see Maryam and Rubiah, and hoped that they, with their life experience and commanding natures, would get Osman back on his feet.

'Come and sit,' she urged them, pulling side tables away from the sofa so they could sit comfortably. 'Osman will be right here. Rahman and Aliza were here just yesterday, or the day before, I can't remember, and it did him a world of good to see friends and start thinking about work again.'

Osman soon tottered into the living room, fully dressed in a sarong and shirt but looking drawn and somehow…old. Maryam sought to hide her surprise – it wouldn't help Osman one bit to have them exclaiming over how ill he looked. They were there for encouragement, and that's what they would supply.

'How are you?' Rubiah sang out, giving him a big smile and proffering her cakes. 'I thought you'd need some to build up your strength.'

He smiled back with as much energy as he could muster and began eating cakes in a mechanical way. 'When are you going back to work?' Maryam asked him.

He looked directly at her and put down the cake he had in his hand. 'It's been difficult,' he said slowly. He knew that courtesy suggested he put as good a face on his condition as possible, and agree he was fine and mending quickly, but seeing Maryam and Rubiah made him want to tell them what was actually happening. He hoped they could help him ... if anyone could it would be these two women.

'Mak Cik,' he began again, 'what happened to me at Omar's house was so strange, so frightening, I still can't really understand what it is. Rahman told me the other bomoh – Deraman, was it? – said he's stealing people's energy and life to give it to his wife. I feel that way. Isn't it strange? But I feel as though some of the life has been sucked out of me and I haven't gotten it back yet.'

'Have you seen Pak Lah?' she asked anxiously. 'You know, these things have to be fought by someone who has the knowledge, not just anyone. I see you've gotten some of your semangat back already. From what I heard, you were unconscious when you got back here, and now you're up.'

'Up, yes, but not much.'

'He didn't want me to call the bomoh,' Azrina interjected. 'I think we should...'

'Of course you should,' Maryam took charge. 'We'll have to get this going right away. Every day we wait we're wasting time.' Osman looked somewhat alarmed at the determination now coming his way. He knew they'd take over the situation, but he wasn't expecting it to be so immediate. Though when he thought more about it he realized he ought to have known better. He sighed, and felt he'd now taken the status of a project which they would complete with him or in spite of him. It was good to know he was in such competent hands, and a bit scary to lose all sense of volition. His life here had been like that.

'I know you feel you don't need this,' Maryam assured him, 'but you do.' She turned to Azrina. 'Let me call Rahman so he can bring Pak Lah here now.' She didn't even glance at Osman now, launching into action. They knew, even if Osman pretended not to, that to fight magic you need magic, otherwise his recuperation would be endless, and it was unclear whether it would be complete. He would be cured, whether he liked it or not.

***

Pak Lah ushered them all onto the porch, leaving Osman sleeping lightly in the living room, looking less haggard than he had been.

'This Omar is really something,' Pak Lah began. 'I'm not sure what he's using but he's draining his victims.'

'That's for his wife,' Rubiah interrupted. 'She's been sick…'

'I heard.'

'…and he's using other people's semangat to pour into her, if that's the right way to describe it.'

'It'll work.'

'Yes, making them zombies.' There, Rubiah had gotten to describe it in her favourite way. 'It's what he's been doing.'

Pak Lah looked serious. 'He could easily hurt people like that.'

'He has,' Maryam assured him. 'You know, using his spells to see how far he can go. He's just killed Hassan, a man in Kampong Laut, who was watching the top-spinning contest. The top just flew up from the ground. How does that happen? And the man who threw it, he's feeling so guilty even though he doesn't really bear responsibility for it. I mean, he threw it but he certainly didn't change it into a weapon. That was Omar.' Maryam nodded for emphasis.

'I'll prepare something for Che Osman to drink,' Pak Lah said thoughtfully. 'Something to strengthen him and give him energy. But we also need to protect him, because this man will strike again. He thinks he's almost got him and I don't think he'll let go.'

'Do you know Deraman, the bomoh in Kampong Laut?' Azrina asked eagerly. 'He knew Omar when they were young and went to talk to him. Omar nearly took his wife! She said she could feel the life slipping out of her and couldn't stop it.'

Pak Lah looked at her and sipped at his coffee. 'Is she alright now?'

Azrina shrugged. 'I think so. I haven't seen them...'

Pak Lah rubbed his forehead pensively. 'I must speak with this Deraman. It might take two of us. In the meantime, I'll leave you with the things you'll need right now.' He began instructing Azrina on what to give her husband and where to place the amulets that would protect his spirit.

Azrina was cheered already, just having Pak Lah examine

Osman and provide help. She feared she wouldn't be able to cure him and couldn't bear the thought of him slipping away from her. Besides, he was going to be badly needed when the baby came.

Chapter XXIV

Deraman was worried on two counts: his wife and Ramli. He had stopped in to see Ramli, just to keep an eye on him. Anyone who'd come into Omar's orbit was in danger, he felt, and though Ramli may have been an unwitting tool, he had still been influenced and Deraman feared Omar might return to him.

He'd noticed Ramli had changed. Right after the accident, he seemed himself: sad, perhaps, and regretful that it had happened, but not guilty about it. That was as it should have been, Deraman thought. But now, it seemed Ramli felt the sin weighed on him, and was bent under it. Deraman had spoken to him, like a father to a son, assuring him that this was not his fault to assume. It was whoever had actually planned it, plotted for it, and that person was not Ramli. But Ramli's listlessness frightened him, making him fear that he too was having his soul taken from him, and Deraman was determined this would not happen again as it had happened to his wife.

He welcomed Pak Lah calling on him and offering to join forces. Pak Lah did not know Omar, and Deraman could provide the background that might help them both fight him.

Pak Lah heard the story, about Jah's illness and her emptiness.

How her only return to this world was through the energy of others, which in turn left them sapped, and as empty as Jah had become. And all their energy, all their life force, only animated Jah for a short time, as though there was hardly enough energy around to keep her soul tied to her body.

'Could her condition be an experiment of his which went badly wrong?' Pak Lah asked after listening intently to Deraman. 'Perhaps that's why he's so frantic about it. Could it be he knows this was his doing and he can't live with it?'

Deraman looked at him a long time. 'I don't know,' he finally said. 'I never thought about that. I just assumed...I just thought it was an illness, you know, just something that happened. I never thought it could be Omar who'd done it.'

'Not that he would have meant to,' Pak Lah added.

'Of course not. He never would have meant to harm her. But what could have happened?'

'Can we find out?'

'We can try. But will it help the people he's injuring now? Does it matter why he's doing it? I mean, whether it's just that his wife is ill or that he's responsible for her condition?'

'I think it does,' Pak Lah answered. 'If we know the basis, we might see how he's doing it. What is the *niat*, the intent? That's so important. I'm not sure, but maybe that would affect how he'd put together his spells ... I feel it's important. This whole experimenting with his jampi with all these athletes, there's something there.

'It's as though I'm seeing it through a fog and I can't see anything clearly yet. But the more we know...'

'The better off we'll be,' Deraman finished. 'You should meet my wife. I was sitting there, and she began to fade. I don't think she remembers that much of it, except that she was slipping away. I haven't been talking to her about it too much because I don't want her upset.' He paused, marshalling his thoughts. 'She'd want to help as much as she can, though. She said it was terrifying and I know she'd want to save other people from the same thing.'

As though summoned by their interest, Anim appeared in the room carrying a tray of coffee and cakes. As she served, Deraman asked, 'Would you mind talking to us about what happened at Omar's house? This is Pak Lah, from Kampong Penambang, he's worked with Kakak Maryam.'

'Are you looking into this case too?'

Pak Lah nodded. 'It's gone too far now. You aren't the only one whose been, how should I say this, attacked? He's been going after people who are looking into the death at the top-spinning contest, just as he did to you, and we're trying to figure out why.'

She sat down with them. 'I'll help. I'd love to see this all end. Even for Jah.' She continued softly. 'He won't let her go, you know. She might prefer to simply leave this world, rather than stay in the state she's in. I know she would. But he can't let her go, so she's kept here, drifting around, because he loves her and can't live without her.'

'How do you know?' Pak Lah asked curiously.

She smiled sadly. 'I nearly lost my own soul to her, you know, at his house. It let me feel some of what she's feeling, I think. Either that, or I've made it up, but I don't think so. I feel something about her…

'I'm not putting it into words very well,' she apologized. 'Well, I never had to describe anything like this either. It's so strange.'

'Tell me,' Pak Lah urged, 'it can be so important to try to stop this.'

Anim nodded. 'I don't know why he does it. No idea at all. But Jah, she's empty inside. *Terlayang-layang bagai bulu sehelai*: blown about like a feather, all alone.

'I don't know what caused it. It's an illness, I suppose. Could it be a jampi? You'd know that better than I would. But the outcome is she's really not there any longer. I can't imagine what it would be to live in that emptiness day in and day out. All alone.' She shuddered. 'You're beyond help, you're in exile, you're isolated. In a crowd of people you're in the wilderness. Am I making sense here? It's as though I can hear a wind howling through her mind, it's hollow, it's dust.'

She thought for a minute and then smiled apologetically. 'I'm sure you don't know what I'm talking about. But I saw it, I felt it at his house. What a terrifying place it is, and poor Jah is wandering there. I can't bear thinking about it.' She sat quietly.

'Kakak Anim, you've described it so well. I didn't know that's what it was. I didn't know anything of the fear you're describing. Thank you.

'I would have thought her mind was perfectly silent. Calm even. But you've told me she's suffering.'

Anim nodded at the two men. 'As I said, it's Omar who won't let her go. When he brings some semangat into her, she can be alive for a time, but even so I think she knows where she'll be falling back to. It's so sad.'

She looked around again and rose. 'I should be leaving you to your discussion. I'm so glad you came, Pak Lah.' She vanished into the kitchen.

'She's very wise, very perceptive,' Pak Lah commented.

'More than I am,' Deraman agreed. 'I'm lucky to have her.'

Pak Lah smiled. 'Her description of what Jah is going through, though: it's a catastrophe. *Putus timba, tinggal tali*: the bucket has dropped and only the cord is left. Has Kakak Anim been alright since that incident?' he asked, changing topics.

Deraman considered it. 'Yes, and no.' He laughed. 'Not very helpful. As you see, she's completely in control of herself and she's thinking perfectly well. But sometimes she seems to me, distant, maybe. As though part of her is missing. I don't know whether I'm imagining it, I certainly could be. But I can't help but watch her very carefully.'

Pak Lah nodded. 'There's another patient I'd like you to see,' he told him. 'Che Osman, the police chief. He was rescued by his men, and his wife, I must add, when he was already unconscious. Kakak Maryam just called me in to take a look at him as he's healing so slowly. Naturally, he didn't want to call me in. From Perak, you see.'

Deraman nodded knowingly.

'But his wife and Kakak Maryam were alarmed and I went to see him. I've put *azimat*, talismans around the house and on him, and told his wife to insist he eats. I'd like you to take a look. Consult on it, like they do in the hospital.'

Deraman grinned. 'I'd be delighted. I think it's time I went hand to hand with Omar and stopped this.'

'His magic is quite strong,' Pak Lah added, almost casually. 'He's very good at what he does, even though I don't think it's worth doing.'

Chapter XXV

At first glance, Osman did not appear to have improved much. He was still tired, still in bed, though Azrina felt he was slowly coming around. She felt much calmer now that Pak Lah was caring for him, and wondered at Osman's reluctance to call him in. Surely he knew even better than she did that an evil bomoh can only be fought with a good one. Cough medicine would simply not cut it.

She hadn't told him yet about the baby, not wanting to overtax his system. She hadn't thought yet about where she'd have the child: to stay in Kelantan or return to Perak? She dearly wanted her parents with her when she gave birth and wanted to discuss it with her husband. Another reason for him to get well quickly!

Pak Lah came back the next day and every day after that, adjusting his protective spells, offering different herbal concoctions, examining his patient. He seemed satisfied with Osman's progress, though of course, he had no news burning to be told. Osman was improving, she could see that, but it was a slow and steady process and she was ready for him to burst out of his lethargy and come back to his usual self.

Pak Lah was giving her considering sort of looks, and finally asked her if she was expecting. She hadn't meant to tell him, but the question brought out all her excitement, and she began to happily describe what was happening.

'Yes, I am! It's our first, you know, so it's really something. I guess everything will change. I don't know if I want to have the baby here or back in Perak, I'd like to have my family with me and help me with the baby. Of course, Osman doesn't know yet, I was afraid to tell him, weak as he is now. Do you think he could take it?' She ended breathlessly.

Pak Lah smiled. 'That's a lot to consider. I think when Osman gets just a little stronger it would be alright to tell him. News like that would lift him, give him a reason to recover even faster.'

'He's going to be fine, isn't he?' Doubt began to shadow her face, erasing the colour which had been there before. 'I mean, this isn't going to last forever.'

Pak Lah demurred. 'I think he'll be better. He's young and strong and Omar was stopped by your quick thinking. He's lucky to have you to look out for him; he's certain brave enough but sometimes it needs to be tempered.'

'I couldn't stand it if he didn't get better,' she said in a trembling voice, all animation now departed. 'Do you remember when Mak Cik Maryam...'

'That was even more dangerous,' Pak Lah answered firmly. 'And now she's fine. Osman will be too.' But he didn't look convinced.

The patient presented himself to the bomoh a few minutes later, getting out of bed at Pak Lah's invitation and shuffling into the living room. The walk from the bed to the sofa seemed to tire him, but he gamely arrived and smiled upon arrival.

'I've got a consulting bomoh coming over,' Pak Lah informed him.

'Like Sherlock Holmes,' Osman commented. Pak Lah looked blank.

'A consulting detective in English stories,' Azrina interjected.

'Yes. This is Pak Deraman from Kampong Laut. He's spoken to Kakak Maryam and Kakak Rubiah, and Aliza's husband.'

'Rahman.'

'Rahman,' he agreed. 'He knew Omar from long ago and Omar nearly overwhelmed his wife. So he's got a reason to want this cleared up. Anyway, he's coming here to see how you are and we're planning out next move.'

Osman nodded and sat quietly in his armchair. He didn't seem to be nodding off, but neither was he particularly present. Azrina tried to engage him in conversation, and she could tell he was making an effort to keep up his end. It made her want to cry.

Deraman arrived only a few minutes later, thankfully, and the two bomoh sat on either side of Osman.

'Did you feel anything when it started?' Deraman asked.

'Yes, like I was fainting, or losing consciousness. I couldn't move, I had no will.'

They both nodded and looked concerned.

'That's what my wife says. Did you see anything in the house?'

'Like what? It was dark. I think he had a kerosene lantern but it only lit part of the room.'

'Like a grasshopper.'

'No. His pelesit? I didn't see one.'

'Another animal perhaps?'

Osman shook his head. 'Maybe Rahman or my other men saw something. They were much more alert that I was at the time. Or now, too.'

'No matter,' Pak Lah interjected. 'You had something to eat or drink?'

'Coffee.'

'Aaaah.' The two bomoh leaned back looking absolutely satisfied. 'Poison,' Pak Lah said. 'Exactly' Deraman concurred. They were thankful that this seemed to at least bring part of the puzzle into the realm of the natural.

'Could that have been the case with others?'

'With Anim it was,' Deraman offered. 'We had coffee. Jah served it.'

'Helping her own cause then?'

Deraman shrugged. 'But it still doesn't explain how that would benefit Jah. Even if Che Osman here was given poison, even if my wife was too, how does that help him? He can make people confused and dizzy, even feel empty and unable to think, but that isn't all he wants.'

'True,' Pak Lah agreed. 'But could it make them more susceptible?'

'What about the other people? Mahmud, even Hassan?'

'They were killed, yes, I think that's the right word, for other reasons. He wasn't draining their energy, he was just murdering them.'

Azrina had been listening closely to the conversation, but this point did not necessarily cheer her. Dead was dead.

'Maybe. But first things first. We need to know what kind of poison so we can cure it.'

'Should we go to speak with him?'

They looked doubtfully at each other, though it was clearly what needed to be done.

***

Ramli was in trouble. He thought so himself. All his certainties had begun to falter. He returned to Deraman at Keri's urging; she'd seen now what Omar could do and she feared the worst for her husband.

Deraman wished he'd been more surprised to see Ramli in his living room, but he'd been expecting it. This was no longer the strapping athlete he'd known and provided with jampi. This Ramli was far more tentative, frightened, fragile. He was thinner and paler, he looked around him every so often as though he expected to find something darting out at him from an unexpected corner. He reminded Deraman of a squirrel on the ground, always casting around to find the danger it may not have yet sensed but knew was out there. The Ramli he'd known had not inhabited the world fearfully as he now did.

Ramli sat quietly, not wringing his hands or complaining about what had happened, but his unease was palpable. 'Pak Deraman,' he began, 'I've come for help. After the accident I knew I hadn't done anything wrong, I had no intention of hurting anyone, and I felt sure the fault was not mine. I still believe that, it was not my fault, but I'm suffering for it nonetheless and I need you to help me.'

'Of course I will.'

'I must be freed from this.' He lowered his voice. 'It will kill me.'

'What will kill you?' Deraman leaned in to hear Ramli whisper.

'He'll send something. He's afraid I know something, but I don't. I have nothing to tell because I don't know anything, but that won't matter. You'll see, I'll be dead, as dead as Hassan, to keep me quiet, but I don't even know about what.' A fine film of sweat appeared on Ramli's upper lip.

Deraman put a comforting hand on his arm. 'I will do all I can to protect you, Ramli, but I need to know exactly what you're talking about.'

'You know,' Ramli replied urgently. 'You know it's Omar. He's after me.'

'Have you seen him?'

Ramli gave him a look of pure annoyance. 'Of course not! I don't have to see him. I know he's there.'

Deraman felt, as he had before, he was hearing dialogue from a horror film. How had things gotten so…weird?

'Omar is coming for you.'

'Yes,' he hissed, 'he's been coming for me and he won't stop until I'm dead and quiet and he doesn't have to worry about me saying anything. But I don't know anything so I can't say anything anyway. I'll die for no reason. What will my family do? I don't even really know him. I never used him for any jampi, thank God. I can't even think what would be happening to me if I had. No, I already know. I'd be dead already. Long ago.' Ramli was starting to babble, but Deraman thought it best to let him continue.

'He used me, he took the top out of my hands and killed Hassan with it. Why Hassan? Such a nice man with no enemies. Why kill him? Why use me?

I'll tell you. He wanted to work through you.' Deraman drew back in shock. 'He knows you, he wanted to get you involved in all this. Kill someone from Kampong Laut, and have the weapon leave the hand of someone from Kampong Laut. It all ends up in your hands, don't you see?'

Deraman wasn't at all sure that he did, but hardly felt it was time to debate it.

'I think you're really the target here,' Ramli continued, spittle accumulating at the corners of his mouth. Now Deraman could see how thin he'd really become. He hadn't been sure he'd believed Ramli before, although he certainly believed he'd been stricken by something. But now, he had to give this credence. This wasn't undirected raving.

'So you think I'm the person Omar's coming after,' he said to Ramli, who nodded, relieved that finally Deraman seemed to be following him. 'And that in staging Hassan's death, through you, both of you being from my own village, I would have to be involved.' Ramli nodded again. Deraman was sure Ramli wondered how he could be so dense. He was beginning to wonder it himself.

'I need to confront Omar, myself,' he concluded, and Ramli led out a relieved sigh.

'Yes,' he said. 'It must be you.' He nodded, more to himself than to Deraman, and then slowly, gracefully, fell over on his side.

***

Rahman tried his best to forget all about the case, at least in the evening. He needed some time away from all this. It was a good thing that Maryam, and everyone else, accepted that Ramli was not to blame, and that Omar bore the responsibility. He didn't believe for a moment that Omar cared about that, but he did believe Omar did not welcome the attention he was getting and was feeling cornered. Though it meant they were making progress, he feared what Omar might do in desperation, and he was sure it would be both petrifying and dangerous. Rahman had seen enough of Omar's actions when he wasn't threatened, and he feared his own family would be at risk if Omar was.

He walked in the door of his house, thrilled to see Aliza there as he was every evening – the novelty hadn't yet worn off, and it was still surprising to see her there casually, as if she lived there. Which of course, she did. Amazing.

'Any news?' she asked as he came into the kitchen. He recognized the recipe as one he'd eaten at her mother's house. Well, that was to be expected.

'Nothing much,' he answered. 'Getting concerned, a little,' he commented, trying to sound offhand. Aliza was having none of it.

'About Omar?' she went right for the target. 'How will you charge him? Is it really a legal matter now or more a, what shall I call it, a bomoh matter? I mean he's evil all right, but has he broken any laws?'

'That's the thing. But I was thinking, maybe we could charge him with attempted murder, for Osman, you know. '

'What about Hassan?'

He frowned. 'I don't know. Would they take such a case, that he killed by jampi? Or would the court refuse to hear it because it isn't the kind of murder they're used to?'

Aliza leaned back against the small table in the middle of the kitchen. 'I imagine they'd say it wasn't a legal case. No lawyer wants to prosecute on jampi. Or on making people into zombies, either.'

'No they don't,' he agreed morosely. 'And that's all we're likely to have.'

'You don't think he might try to actually help it along? Try to physically kill someone, do you?'

'Why?' he asked, still dejected. 'The jampi seem to be working beautifully. I don't see why he'd have to add anything to it, do you? People are already falling like flies. Or becoming zombies, or whatever that is.' He picked up a raw string bean and began to chew it ruminatively. 'Could we, I don't know, encourage him to move in a regular way against someone?'

'Entice him into murder?' Aliza asked blandly. 'Why not?'

Rahman made a face at her. 'When you put it like that…'

'It sounds bad,' she finished for him. 'Because it is. He doesn't need any encouragement, he's already a one-man disaster.'

He examined his string bean and picked up another. 'I want to catch him before he hurts someone else. I wonder if Ramli would help me. He looked like the kind of guy who'd want to help out.' Aliza said nothing. There wasn't anything to say about it, but she thought it unlikely Ramli wanted to tangle with the dark arts any time soon.

'I should talk to him. See what he thinks. Do you want to come?'

Aliza looked doubtful. 'Is it fair to ask him to do anything like that? It could be very dangerous for him. We should leave him alone,' she admonished Rahman. 'Please. I really don't think…'

'I could just talk to him. I won't be asking him to do anything.'

Aliza did not quite believe this. 'Just talking to him about it might make him feel pressured…'

'No pressure,' Rahman answered firmly. 'Just a talk.'

Aliza shook her head and returned to the coconut milk. 'I'll come with you,' she agreed. 'Just to make sure you don't make him miserable.'

Chapter XXVI

Rahman and Aliza were shocked to see Ramli. His shirt hung from his bony shoulders, and his sarong could have fit another man comfortably inside it. And this was a man who'd not long ago had been a well-known athlete, fit and strong. Ramli well knew what he looked like, even though his visitors both tried to hide their surprise.

'He's after me,' Ramli began, just as Keri was serving tea and looking worried. 'Omar. You know that, right? He's killing me, because he thinks I know something that I can tell you. I don't know anything but I'm going to die for it anyway.'

Keri looked stricken, and sat down next to her husband, keeping her eyes on him, urging him wordlessly to eat something. Rahman opened his mouth to speak but words failed him. How could he have thought to ask this man to put himself in any more danger than he was already in? He took a quick look at Aliza and saw she was clearly thinking the same thing.

'What can we do to help?' Aliza asked. 'What would you like us to do? This can't continue. You must eat, Che Ramli. You mustn't give up.'

His wife nodded. 'She's right, you have to eat.'

'I can't,' Ramli explained, looking at Rahman. 'I just can't put any food in my mouth.'

'You've got to fight it,' Rahman urged him. 'Don't let anyone do this to you. Even if you don't want to, think of it as a gesture against Omar, a way of not allowing him to take over your life. You're strong. Even if you choke down the food, it's still better than accepting this fate, isn't it?'

Ramli shook his head slowly. 'It's my fate. He's killing me because he thinks I know something, or Che' Hassan is killing me because he blames me for his death. Either way, I'm going to meet him soon.'

Keri looked aghast.

'You can talk to Hassan's family,' Aliza told him. 'They don't blame you at all. They'll tell you they hold nothing against you: no grudges, no anger. A main puteri curing ceremony, that's what you need. With Hassan's family there to make it clear this is not your doing.' She was speaking very quickly now, as if she feared Ramli might not survive until the end of her sentence. 'Please, we can help you arrange that,' she said, mostly to Keri, who sat silently. 'What do you think? Pak Deraman will help, I know he will...'

'Yes,' Keri answered firmly. 'That might help. Whatever spirits are being sent, that would get rid of them.' She and Aliza stood, as though of one mind. 'We'll go to Deraman now,' Keri said, the light of battle coming on in her eyes. 'We'll get this organized quickly.'

When they left, Rahman turned to Ramli. 'It's out of our hands now, you know. They'll have a main puteri organized before you know what's happened.'

Ramli gave him a sickly smile. 'That's Kelantan women for you,. When they decide to do something there's no point in fighting it. I guess we're having a ceremony. Do you think it will help?' he asked Rahman, as though asking for reassurance.

'It can't hurt,' he replied.

***

The main puteri ceremony would be talked about in Kampong Laut long after the last spectator had left this world. Student bomoh would be taught about it, and anyone who returned from college in the United States or the United Kingdom professing a disbelief in spirits would be presented with it as Exhibit A in how they existed in Kelantan, if not on other continents.

Deraman and Pak Lah worked in tandem during the ceremony, and a good thing, too: at least two bomoh were needed to corral the troop of evil spirits, pelesit, *hantu*, familiars and heaven only knows what other kinds of creatures of darkness who decided to attend or had been sent by their owner.

Maryam decided to sit towards the back of the crowd, unwilling to be too close to the action lest she be inspired by it and perhaps possessed. She'd been before, at a ceremony held for her, and believed it made her susceptible to its influence. She watched anxiously as it began, slowly and quietly at first, while the bomoh spoke to the spirits as they presented themselves. At first, it seemed the spirit world was on its best behaviour, answering politely, making jokes and in general behaving as guests should.

And then, he arrived.

It was as though a thick shadow came over the area, rendering it dark and difficult to see. Pak Deraman seemed disoriented, even anxious, and the voice which now poured out of him was definitely not his. It was deep, loud and gravelly, and it spoke the unspeakable, threatening the bomoh and everyone who watched, bringing Deraman to his unsteady feet and flinging him around the dancing area. Pak Lah tried to grasp him, to keep him from hurting himself, but he was thrown off as the spirit refused to brook any interference in his possession of the bomoh. Deraman was dashed to the ground and then lifted up again, like a kitten in the mouth of its mother, only to be dropped hard once more and stamped into the dust. Deraman's wife, Anim, leaped to her feet and tried to reach him, and she was felled onto the ground, and lay there motionless. People around her were afraid to pick her up, lest they too be beaten, and mayhem ensued.

Maryam reached for Mamat, who held her arm tightly, and tried to guide them both away from the audience. Since they were already in the back, he hoped they could leave without attracting notice, but they could not. Deraman roared at them, demanding they stop, and when Mamat kept going, Maryam was yanked back by an unseen hand. It had taken firm hold of her hair, tearing it out of her bun and threatening to rip it out of her head. She screamed, and Mamat threw himself over her to protect her, but the spirit would not be appeased or distracted. As though she were outside of herself, Maryam noted it seemed able to torture her while still keeping a firm grip on Deraman.

She lay in the dust, afraid to move, unsure as to whether she could move at any rate, listening to what sounded like a howling wind with screaming within it. Pak Lah was desperately shouting questions at the spirit, trying to find its name and what it wanted. It wasn't answering, and Maryam thought what it wanted was to cause panic and maybe death. The usual offerings of water and rice and perhaps flowers were of no interest to it – it would not be bought off.

'Are you Omar?' Pak Lah finally screamed as loud as he could, goading the spirit to answer him and let go of Deraman. It laughed, one of the most terrifying sounds anyone in the audience had ever heard. Horror movie soundtracks had never imagined such a laugh, filled with hate and malice, a preening, arrogant laugh which rejoiced in the spirit's triumph over the humans at the ceremony. Maryam heard a deep rumble, as though the earth itself were speaking, but couldn't make out anything intelligible. Pak Lah apparently could, because he continued his conversation with it.

While he spoke, the area became even darker and now a wind came up, moaning over the heads of the people sitting. It was as though hell had opened up below them and taken up residence in Kampong Laut.

Chapter XXVI

Maryam could not remember how she got home, and Mamat changed the subject every time it was brought up. She'd been hurt, as had many people watching the ceremony: a trove of broken bones, bad bruises and post-traumatic stress syndrome was found throughout Kampong Laut, which did not recover its collective equilibrium for weeks after the event.

The most serious of these was borne by Ramli, who was found in the morning under a collapsed shed. He'd died sometime during the night, a victim, Pak Lah averred, of evil intent and even more evil spirits unleashed. The physical cause of death was unclear: his back was purple with bruises and several long cuts, but the bomoh did not think that would have been enough to kill him. Pak Lah and Deraman felt personally responsible for planning the ceremony, even though they had done so out of the best motives possible. Maryam knew intellectually that they had tried their best to help Ramli, and she acknowledged that. Nevertheless, she could not find it in herself to comfort Pak Lah with platitudes about how no one was to blame for what happened, and that no one could have foreseen the horrors set free. Maybe someone, an expert in such matters, should have foreseen it and thereby avoided it.

Pak Lah visited Maryam, ostensibly to check on her injured arm and several ugly gashes to her legs, but in truth he was hoping she could offer him absolution of sorts and convince him that he had not delivered Ramli to whatever dark forces threatened him. Maryam had no absolution to offer and remained badly shaken.

Rubiah took over the bulk of the care, bustling in and out of Maryam's house, encouraging Mamat, bringing enormous quantities of food and lecturing Maryam now that she had her in a weakened state.

'You didn't see me going to Kampong Laut, did you?' she'd demanded after the affair. 'No. But you always have to chase danger!' Her anxiety over Maryam's injuries led her to be far more abrasive than she otherwise would have been. She wanted to shake Maryam for getting herself hurt, for refusing to back away from what she considered her duty. 'This is where it's gotten us! You in pieces!' Maryam lifted her hand as if to dispute that characterization, but Rubiah completely ignored her. 'Ramli: dead! Even the two bomoh look sick to me. *Pucat lesi macam ayam kena lengit:* as pale as a hen plagued by ticks. They'd both best be careful if they don't want to be eaten up themselves by this…thing. Whatever it is.

'Grown people!' she continued, working herself into a fury. 'But no one has the sense to leave this stuff alone. Can't you see what's right in front of you? He's playing for keeps!'

'Who is?' Ashikin asked, walking in the door. She was in charge of the stall while her mother recuperated, while her cousin Puteh, Rubiah's daughter, watched her children. Personally, she thought she'd gotten the easier job, but Puteh had volunteered, perhaps without knowing how imperious Noraini had actually become. Puteh might set her straight though: she had even less patience for that kind of behaviour than Ashikin had herself, which meant essentially none at all.

'Omar!' Rubiah exploded. 'He's going to kill everyone he can find! And your mother won't leave it alone. She has to put herself in danger when the spirits are called up...' Rubiah spluttered to a halt, her anger making her unable to put a sentence together.

'Of course he's playing for keeps,' Ashikin agreed briskly. 'We all knew that already. I guess we've found the killer.'

'He's killed again,' Rubiah said bitterly. 'Ramli. The man who threw the top. He died last night in that bloodbath at Kampong Laut.'

Ashikin now looked concerned. 'Isn't there anything the police can do?'

'I'd rather Rahman stayed out of it,' Maryam said tiredly. The effort to talk was completely wearing her out, as was the effort of listening to Rubiah berate her. 'Osman's still recovering, and I don't want anything to happen to Rahman and maybe Aliza, too.'

'You can't always control what other people do,' Ashikin observed, offering her mother a cake with an attitude that dared her not to eat it. Maryam did not reply, but obediently chewed.

'No, she can't, but she thinks she can. Do you know what happened?'

'Only the gossip,' Ashikin replied. 'I was hoping you could tell me.'

'Ask your father,' Rubiah advised her. 'He was there but

managed to get away with fewer injuries. I guess Omar's spirits were more interested in your mother. He knows her.' She crossed her arms and looked down at Maryam. 'Now are you happy?' she asked rhetorically.

'The whole village can hear you,' Mamat informed her as he came in from the porch. Disaster or not, the birds still needed to be fed. Rubiah would gladly take care of Maryam and Yi, and even Mamat himself, but she drew the line at birds.

'I don't care,' Rubiah told him. He was astonished to hear such sentiment from the usually decorous Rubiah. 'Maybe if I'm loud enough your wife will also hear me.'

'Maybe,' Ashikin said, without much confidence.

'My legs hurt,' Maryam said weakly. She was tired of being harangued, and the cuts on her legs burned. 'Can you put the medicine on them?'

Ashikin prepared to cover them in salve. 'So tell me what happened.'

Mamat didn't know where to start. It wasn't that clear to him what happened, and even less could he express it to Ashikin. But he'd try.

'The main puteri started, quietly enough, as they usually do. Deraman was working with the spirits, Pak Lah was there to protect him.' Rubiah snorted. 'And then, after the back and forth, you know, with jokes and so forth, suddenly, everything turned dark.' He became more dramatic. 'It was night, of course, but it was a thicker darkness, as though we were enveloped in a black cloud. You couldn't see very well, but I think everyone could feel the danger. The ceremony shifted, Deraman couldn't control the spirits, they were too strong.

'But even more than that, they weren't interested in any offerings or dancing, or any of the things they usually want. These were bent on killing Ramli, I think, and injuring as many people as they could. We were sitting at the edge of the crowd, so we could leave quickly if we had to. We had to. I was holding on to your mother, and the spirit reached out and grabbed her by the hair. You could see how tightly he was holding it, and how much it hurt her. She was thrown to the ground in the midst of the crowd, which by now was panicking and trying to get away, but the darkness became even thicker and people were trapped. How they began cutting people I don't know, but a lot of people were beaten and cut, legs broken, arms broken. An unseen spirit,' he began to speak more quickly now, reliving the event, becoming uneasy about even talking about the spirits. 'I tried to find your mother; I was crawling on the ground, because everyone who had been standing had been smacked down. The ground was covered with people, crying, moaning, hurt. I've never seen anything like it.

'I heard Deraman shouting at the spirit. I couldn't understand what he was saying. Pak Lah was holding the back of his sarong, he was shouting too, but it seemed to me the dark was swirling around them, you could hear the wind. They kept struggling, and then...I don't remember. Really I don't. I knew Ramli was dead, but I don't know how I did because I didn't see him. We must have taken the ferry back to Kampong Penambang because here we are, but I don't remember getting on it or coming back to the house. The first thing I remember was early this morning, we were back and you were here,' he indicated Rubiah, 'helping us. How did you know to come over?'

Rubiah looked confused. 'I, well I, got up in the morning and thought I'd better check on you and see what happened during the ceremony. When I left my house I heard people talking about the horrors at Kampong Laut, so I came here as fast as I could.'

Ashikin nodded. 'The whole market was buzzing. I went to open your stall, because I know that's what you would want me to do, and Puteh said she'd go to pick up the kids from Daud's parents.' She reflected for a moment. 'I know what you mean, Mak Cik Rubiah, I heard about it, but I kind of knew it, too. Before I heard. Does that make any sense?'

Rubiah nodded. 'As much as anything else here makes sense, yes. What a story! I've never heard of spirits erupting like that.'

'Like a volcano,' Ashikin murmured. 'Like they were shot out of a cannon.'

'It's all confused,' Maryam began speaking softly. It hurt to speak; it hurt to breath but she felt her side of the story had to be told, or be forever lost. Perhaps she'd forget it herself soon, what with the whirling in her mind and the memories coming in and out of focus. She tried to concentrate, and it exhausted her.

'The beginning, as Ayah said, was the usual main puteri, people talking and jokes being made and even snacks sold, like they always are. I wonder what happened to the stalls there…'

'Knocked over. Destroyed,' Mamat muttered.

'And …' Ashikin prompted her.

'And then, Deraman was possessed. An evil, evil spirit, looking for blood. Bringing death!' she added theatrically. 'It got darker, really dark, not like night but like, well, being inside a black sarong wrapped around you. You couldn't see through this dark. A wind came up from nowhere and started whistling around our ears. Your father and I tried to move away and then suddenly, I felt a hand pulling my hair as if it was going to pull it right out of my head. My bun came out,' it was odd how this completely unimportant detail remained with her. Perhaps fixing upon this would wipe out the memory of everything else that happened, but it wasn't working. 'I was pulled back toward the centre of everything by my hair. I think I was screaming. I heard screaming anyway, it could have been me; it could have been other people. I don't know,' she ended hopelessly.

'It was horrible. I couldn't see. I didn't know where I was. My hair was coming out of my head and I felt my legs being cut. Just like a *parang* was slicing my legs. Like I was a piece of meat. I think,' she paused. 'I think, but I'm not sure, a lot of people were being cut. It seemed to me there was a lot of blood on the ground, but it was so dark,' her words were coming faster now, 'I didn't really know what was happening. I was so scared. I could hear shouting and crying but I couldn't tell where it was coming from. I was lost in a cyclone, that's what it was like, and I could hear the moans of people hurt and dying and I didn't know where they were.' She started to cry and Mamat sat next to her holding her hand.

'There now,' he said. 'You're home and safe and you don't need to be frightened anymore.'

'But my legs,' she sobbed. 'These aren't just cuts, they're magical cuts, they're cursed. I don't know if I'll ever get better.'

Ashikin and Rubiah exchanged a look, and even Rubiah could not find the heart to berate Maryam again. Or rather to berate her out loud, since she was definitely doing so silently and wondered if she'd ever stop.

'Mak,' Ashikin said briskly, 'of course they'll heal. It might take a little time, but Pak Lah will make sure…'

'Pak Lah is out of his depth,' Maryam said forcefully, surprising even herself. Did she really feel that way? She supposed she did, since it burst out of her like that. 'I mean,' she continued tiredly, 'I think this is something even he's having trouble understanding. Otherwise he would have controlled it when it started, and he wasn't able to.'

'I think we might go to Dr. Bates,' Ashikin continued, pretending not to have heard what her mother said. If she thought about it too much, she too might succumb to despair, and then who would take care of everyone?

'You like him,' Ashikin said hopefully, 'and he's such a good doctor. Why don't we let him take a look?'

***

Dr. Bates had his dispensary near the market and was an Englishman who'd lived in Kelantan for his whole professional life. He'd been the doctor they'd gone to if ailments were clearly not in the realm of the bomoh and needed antibiotics, or in times of real emergency. Maryam had been to him several years earlier when she'd stepped on a jampi placed under her stairs with a poisoned catfish spine sticking out from it, and Dr. Bates had taken quick action, which had saved her.

She was now carried back into the dispensary with an escort of Mamat, Abdullah, Rubiah and Ashikin, all of whom went directly to his nurse, Poh Choo, to make sure she understood the urgency of the visit. When Poh Choo looked down at Maryam's sarong and saw blood seeping into it, she was alarmed, and ushered Maryam into an examination room without further discussion.

Dr. Bates, famed for speaking only the absolute minimum number of words necessary, moved the sarong aside and stared at the cuts on the legs. They were still oozing blood and looked red and angry. 'What's this?' he asked as if the words were jerked out of him. 'What happened?'

Mamat began to explain. 'Kampong Laut?' Dr. Bates interrupted. 'I heard about that. Everyone's talking. What a disaster. I've seen some people here already with injuries. What was put in these cuts?'

'Just some salve,' Ashikin said, bringing out the rest of the tube to show him. 'From the drug store.'

'Was there something on the knife? Poison or anything?'

Maryam shook her head, suddenly gasping for air. 'I don't know. I don't even know who did it.'

He nodded, seemingly unsurprised. Apparently he'd heard similar stories all morning.

He touched the cuts gingerly and Maryam hissed through her teeth. 'It hurts?' he said more than asked, and she nodded, not trusting herself to speak. She kept her eyes fixed on the wall across from her, afraid to look at her legs.

'I'm going to clean them,' he said, not unkindly. 'It's going to hurt. Let me give you something to make you drowsy.'

'I'm fine,' she said. 'I can manage.'

'No, you can't,' he said gently. 'You have no idea what you're in for.'

He gave her some pills and some tea, and while she struggled to stay awake the medicine and her own fatigue overcame her, and she drifted off. The doctor turned to Mamat and Abdullah. 'Even though she's not conscious, she might feel this. I need you to hold her legs so I can clean the cuts. Hold tight – I want to do this as quickly as possible.'

He raised his eyebrows at them, and each clamped onto an ankle, trying to think of something other than the woman lying in front of him. Poh Choo came into the room to assist, and she and Dr. Bates worked quickly, cleaning the cuts and bringing out what seemed to be dirt, which her family was seeing for the first time, and which Rubiah swore had not been there when she'd cleaned Maryam up earlier that morning. Suddenly, Maryam started convulsing, throwing her legs around and would have fallen off the table had not the two men been holding fast.

'Hold on!' the doctor cried to them as he pressed against the cuts and refused to be put off. Rubiah and Ashikin moved forward to hold her arms, and Maryam moaned and made noises which sounded like speech but were unintelligible. They all began to sweat, and Dr. Bates worked to finish the procedure.

'She's possessed,' Rubiah whispered to Ashikin, who refused to acknowledge hearing her.

In a few minutes, the cuts were cleaned, and blackened gauze lay all over the floor of the room. As the procedure stopped, Maryam became quiet, and they were able to loosen their grip on her. Poh Choo leaned against the wall and buried her face in a towel, breathing hard. Dr. Bates was gulping air but looked relieved.

'We did it. I think whatever poison that might have been is out. Look at this,' he waved at the floor, gasping. Do you see all that? That's not dirt. That's something else. I'm putting medicine on the cuts and I'll cover them. I'll send you home with some and it should be reapplied morning and evening.'

He began to recover his poise. He wiped his forehead and sighed. 'She always has the most interesting ailments.'

Chapter XXVII

'We've failed,' Pak Lah told Deraman. 'I should get out of this business. What have I accomplished? Poor Ramli is dead, Hassan is dead ...'

'You had nothing to do with that,' Deraman reminded him.

'... and so many people have been hurt. And stampeded,' he continued, ignoring the interruption. 'Did we accomplish anything good? No, we did not. Omar's beaten us,' he said dejectedly. 'I might as well go over there and offer my semangat to him to use for his wife. That's how much use I am.'

Deraman had actually been berating himself in the same way but hearing Pak Lah express it made him want to argue the point. 'We've brought Omar into the open.'

'Are you crazy? He was in the open already! There was no need to make it more public, more terrifying. He's the evil King of Kelantan now, thanks to us. I think I should move away and hide myself. No one will ever trust me again. No one should.'

He slumped against the wall of house, staring off the porch. His wife brought them tea and cigarettes and shot them worried looks but returned into the house. She knew when there was no point getting involved.

'Was Hassan's family there?' he asked Deraman, who looked uncomfortable.

'His daughter, Ibtisam. I saw her at the beginning. I hope she left before…before it all happened.'

'We should make sure she's alright. And Keri. Poor thing, a widow so young. And my fault, too. Maybe we should see them today. I can't be any more miserable than I am now, or more guilty.'

'You won't be much help to them like this,' his wife's voice floated out to them from the house. 'If you aren't strong for them, why visit them?' She appeared in the doorway, hands on her hips. 'Are you waiting for them to make you feel better?' she asked. 'Is that your job?' She glared at both of them.

'*Kita semua mati, tapi kubur masing-masing*: we all die, but each has his own grave. This is your fate! You are bomoh! You owe it to these people to help. You tried, and it didn't work as you'd planned. Alright. Now get up and keep going!' Exasperated, she threw down the cloth she was holding and marched back into the house.

The two men looked at each other somewhat sheepishly. 'I don't know if she understands how serious this is,' Pak Lah said slowly, embarrassed in front of Deraman but knowing his wife was right, much though it pained him. He was shocked she would have berated him like that in public, it simply wasn't done. But perhaps she felt it important enough to give both of them a psychological shove, and damn politeness. Well, she had a point. Still.

Deraman looked at Pak Lah from under his brows. 'Are you

able to go to Kampong Laut today? Maybe we should start again.'

'Start again?'

'I mean, help the people involved. I'm not talking about spirits now. Just the victims, you know. The wives, the children. We can help them get through this. Are you coming with me?' He stood up.

Pak Lah looked confused, then exhausted. 'I don't know if I have the energy,' he admitted softly. 'I just don't know. Maybe I'm too old for this. Maybe I don't have the courage.' He shook his head. 'I'm in over my head.' He looked down at the floor, somewhat ashamed.

'Never,' Deraman said shortly. 'Get on the back of my motorcycle and we're going. Otherwise your wife will never let you hear the end of it. You know that's true.'

Pak Lah sighed. Sadly Deraman was correct. He had no choice.

***

Ibtisam greeted them on the porch of the house, where she sat folding laundry while watching the baby sleep.

'He looks happy,' Deraman greeted her, looking her over quickly to see if she had any injuries. 'He looks bigger.'

'People say he's growing well,' Ibtisam said modestly. 'I don't know…'

Pak Lah came up behind Deraman and smiled at her. 'Were you at the ceremony?' he asked, eschewing small talk on the theory he might as well get it over with as quickly as possible.

She nodded quietly. 'Not at the end though. I left as soon as I thought it was getting darker. Does that sound strange? Everyone's talking about the dark cloud that covered the spot. I saw it and it frightened me. I have a small baby at home, I can't take chances like that. When I saw, I don't know how to describe it, a dark wind surrounding us, I got up and went home right away.'

'A lot of other people wish they had,' Pak Lah observed.

'Yes,' she said simply, looking over at her son, asleep in the shade. 'Such power,' she murmured. 'Such malevolence. I'm not surprised he could kill my father like that. I don't know how the rest of us are still alive.'

'Was anyone else in the family hurt?' Deraman asked.

She shook her head. 'I was the only one there. We stayed in the house while we heard all the noise: the wind, the screaming. We should have come out to help but we were scared, I'll admit it. We've had enough to scare us lately, as you can see.'

The two bomoh nodded sadly. 'You have.' Deraman agreed. 'I'm so sorry. I feel like I made it worse.'

'You did what you had to,' she answered and sighed. 'I appreciate what you've tried to do for us.'

'We must succeed,' Pak Lah said, 'not just try.'

'It's the best you can do,' she said.

Pak Lah had been feeling much like that himself not an hour ago but hearing someone else say it piqued his pride. He would not be the man who just tried and then gave up. He would be the man who succeeded in ridding the world of this evil. It was his destiny.

Chapter XXVIII

There were mutterings in Kampong Laut. It was one thing to frighten people, but another to overawe them utterly. When the first terror had passed, the injuries tallied and Ramli laid to rest, the villagers began to plan their retaliation. They would not live in fear of Omar, for no one had any doubts it was he who brought the dark wind and delivered ghouls to their doorsteps.

Deraman naturally became the focal point for the resistance, since he was both a bomoh and someone who actually knew Omar personally. They turned to him for help in planning what was to be done, though he himself wasn't very sure about it. He feared fighting magic with magic, since Omar clearly spent a lot more time thinking about it and how to use than anyone else he knew, including any other bomoh in Kelantan. Nevertheless, he would have to find some way of neutralizing him, since he'd now become so strong, he could hold all Kelantan in his thrall. The idea brought him back to Rubiah's zombie movies and a general creeping of the skin.

Anim encouraged him to err on the side of courage. She knew first-hand what more people could be in for if Omar wasn't stopped. She considered the body count: Hassan, Ramli, Osman injured, Maryam injured, and a whole host of villagers wounded as well. How did it get to this, she wondered? And though she would never admit it to Deraman, she was as afraid as anyone else.

The Kota Bharu Police were not inactive either. Osman was determined to recover enough to lead his men against this existential threat, both for his professional reputation and to keep the world safe for the baby he'd just heard was coming. He wished he'd been stronger so he could have shown Azrina just how delighted he really was; his reaction had been muted only because he was still so lethargic. But internally, he was jumping up and down and waving flags. He'd yearned for his own child and the excitement served to accelerate his recovery. He walked slowly, still, but he walked. He spoke softly, but he spoke, and no longer spent all day in bed, though he still occasionally wished he could. He could see the encouragement his men offered when he returned to work, and he could not abandon the effort now, when they were girding for battle.

Rahman had stepped back a little when Osman came back to work. He'd been in charge while he was gone but was careful not to overstep and have Osman feel he was not respected because of his weakened state.

Rahman was ready to fight, though Aliza was quite uneasy about it, fearing that her husband might be the next injury when he came to Omar's attention again. She believed Omar would work his way down his list of anyone he'd ever spoken to and make them all miserable, or worse. She'd started thinking about having a baby herself, hearing about Azrina and seeing her little nephews and nieces, and Omar seemed to constitute a significant threat to those plans.

You can't wait forever, she told herself, and though she was hardly on the cusp of forever, she felt it could sneak up on her while her attention was elsewhere, as does so much of life. She hadn't mentioned it to anyone, though Ashikin, in her uncanny way, seemed already to know it and began giving her pregnancy advice. When Aliza protested she wasn't pregnant and therefore didn't need the information, Ashikin looked at her with both annoyance and amusement and said nothing. How did she do it? Aliza had no doubt she already knew the sex of her first three children before she even knew whether she'd have three children, and probably could tell her how they'd do in high school. Aliza avoided the topic in order to leave herself some surprises.

And Maryam, who was one of the first to join into this battle, was still laid up at home, with cuts which were extremely slow to heal, making walking painful and unsteady. She was, she thought, looking as bad as Yi had in the worst of his adolescence, when she'd rush in front of him to get breakables out of his way as he listed dangerously near cabinets and tables. At least Yi seemed to be growing out of it, unless she was actually getting used to it and so didn't notice it as much as she had. Still, he hadn't broken anything lately so perhaps he had really improved, just in time for her to take over the role.

She tried, she really did. Every day she sought to ignore the pain in her legs and in her back and try to walk to strengthen the muscles. And so far, every day she managed to get to the bottom of the stairs into the yard in order to be attacked by geese was a triumph. She'd stand there smiling, pleased with the effort she'd made and fed up with the geese who never seemed to recognize her, though they saw her every day. And each time they were alarmed anew and ready to defend the house against the person who paid for their food. Having pretty much exhausted herself in getting down the stairs, she now had to go up and this trip was always far less triumphant than the first, often necessitating Mamat's help and collapsing on the couch. The next day, she'd try it again, and so her week passed.

'We should get rid of those geese,' she grumbled to Mamat after a particularly spirited attack.

He shook his head. 'We got them for protection, remember? I think they do a great job, and I wouldn't take the chance of being without them.'

'You're the bird expert,' she said between her teeth as she hauled herself up the last step and tottered towards a chair. 'Can't you train them to recognize me?'

'I don't think anyone can train them at all,' Mamat replied, smoothing back her hair which was threatening to come undone. 'Would you like some tea?'

She nodded and smiled, but it was a tired smile, full of pain and frustration. She couldn't imagine living the rest of her life like this, just about able to walk from one end of the house to the other provided she didn't need to carry anything. How would she go back to work? If she hadn't hated Omar before this, she certainly hated him now. He'd crippled her, and she'd never forgive him for it. She was alive, that was true, but how alive was she really? Just one attempt to get into the yard in order to be pecked by geese finished her for the day. And even after she was back and sitting down, she still felt the aching in her legs and the soreness in her arm. She was of no use to anyone anymore.

And Rubiah, who had foreseen the mayhem Omar would bring on them all, and whose warnings had been ignored or mocked, was deeply worried. She'd told them all about the zombies they were in danger of becoming, about the threat Omar posed to them all, and no one listened. It was a curse to know what was coming and have no one pay attention until it was far too late. She saw how difficult it was for Maryam to recover and wondered whether these cuts and bruises were somehow imbued with the supernatural, which prevented them mending. She said nothing to Maryam or Mamat, having said it all before, but she had slipped over to Pak Lah's house and confided her fears to him.

Pak Lah, thankfully, did not laugh at her. He stroked his chin and looked off far into the distance while thinking about what she'd said. 'You know,' he said slowly, still looking at something no one else could see, 'I thought about that. After all, cuts heal, don't they? And these, well, nothing much is happening and that's not natural. Not infected though,' he commented. 'I'm sure Dr. Bates got whatever was in there out. They've stayed clean, haven't they?'

'There must be something you can put on them,' Rubiah interrupted his reverie. 'A salve, a poultice, something.'

He now looked sharply at her. 'Do you think I haven't tried?' he asked with temerity. 'Do you think I've just been sitting here waiting to see…'

'No, of course not,' she assured him, unhappy at provoking

the one person who'd been taking her seriously. 'I don't mean that. I only mean, well…' and she thought about what it was she did mean. 'You know how concerned I am about her and I just want her to get better. I know you can help her. You might be the only one who can.'

He seemed less annoyed now. 'Of course I'd been thinking about it. Perhaps more charms around the house.' Rubiah nodded, encouraging him to keep thinking. 'Something to drink, some water in which I've put a prayer.'

'Yes! That would work!'

'We can try. I hate these things. They should be natural, straightforward, and then, who knows what's going on?' He sat silently for a few moments and then rose. 'Come with me,' he ordered. 'Let me go and see her.'

***

They found Maryam drinking tea in the living room, still ruminating about the geese and what could be done to curb them. It was preferable to thinking about why her legs still hurt or what new torture Omar had in store for them all. She brightened to see Pak Lah and Rubiah.

'Come in, come in,' she invited them. 'Let me get you something to drink…'

Rubiah waved her away and went straight into the kitchen to put up some coffee and rummaged around for the cakes she'd left early in the morning. Get something to drink indeed. Maryam could barely walk; the picture she conjured of Maryam carrying a tray of hot liquid made her wince.

Pak Lah dispensed with small talk. 'We need to do more about your legs,' he said, noticing a glimmer of fear appearing in her eyes.

'Is it that bad?' she stammered. 'That is, I know it's bad, but you don't think it's going to get better anyway? Do you think I'll be like this forever?' It was all she could do not to cry.

'No, no, no,' Pak Lah sought to reassure her. 'I'd just be happier if we could move it along faster, you know. Get you back on your feet in a shorter time. It just seems to me it's taking a long time.'

'Longer than it should,' Maryam corrected him.

'Maybe,' he admitted. 'But that doesn't mean we can't get it better. No! It may mean I haven't been doing enough.'

It was sweet the way Pak Lah took the blame for this, hoping it wouldn't scare her. But she saw it for what it was, and while Pak Lah pretended it was only his concern that he do more, she in turn pretended she believed that was the problem, and not that her wounds were cursed and would never be cured. Both tried to reassure the other, and at least publicly it looked like they agreed. Privately they might have agreed as well, but to a completely different proposition.

'I'm going to put some more jampi around the house, and draw some on your leg,' he began. 'Not where it will hurt,' he added when he saw her flinch. 'Don't worry. Prayers, charms. Protective things. And I'll get some more of the medicine from Dr. Bates. I want you freed from this completely,' he said sternly, as though she had argued with him. 'This has gone on long enough.'

She agreed wholeheartedly. Rubiah returned from the kitchen bearing food and drink and looking quite satisfied, which led Maryam to believe she'd overheard their conversation and agreed with it.

'*Reba menanti api,* the timber awaits the fire,' Pak Lah muttered, vowing to be Omar's nemesis. 'What he's done must be corrected and punished. No sin like that can go…unnoticed.'

Rubiah nodded with satisfaction.

Chapter XXIX

While the disastrous healing ceremony in Kampong Laut galvanized those who sought to curb Omar, it also galvanized Omar himself. He seemed busier than usual, had there been anyone to notice. Of course, Jah was there, but what Jah noticed or not was a matter of conjecture, and she certainly gave no sign that she was aware of Omar at all. His other neighbours gave him a wide berth and pretended not to see him when they were forced to pass his house. However, with no woman to care for it the yard had become seriously overgrown, and most passers-by could plausibly claim to be unable to see the porch itself where Omar so diligently laboured.

The overgrown yard could be a metaphor for all that had gone wrong in Omar's life. It cut him off from his fellows, and made his home and existence seem secret, hidden, and therefore suspect. It did not appear to bother him, however, and he seemed content, even excited, as he bent over his work, occasionally commenting to Jah who sat at the corner of the porch, her eyes focused on nothing. She never replied or acknowledged him, and it was unclear whether she even heard him. Still, Omar seemed content to continue speaking to her, even laughing at her non-existent replies, encouraging her to keep talking. It was a situation guaranteed to make the hair stand up on anyone's neck who witnessed it, and it seemed that people knew it without anything being said as they strenuously avoided the house and its inhabitants.

It was just after dawn, and Omar was already sitting cross-legged in front of the door on his small porch, with Jah on the top step, rigid and silent. Omar had not gotten up early, he hadn't been to bed at all so was just continuing his evening chores. He giggled to himself, bantering with Jah, or himself, really, and working on a jampi he intended to place under the stairs of someone's house. He made no mention of who he intended it for, nor did he hint anything to Jah. He carefully bent over his composition-book sized scrap of yellow cloth, onto which he was painstakingly drawing designs and pictures which might lead anyone who stepped over it to fall over, hopefully breaking their necks in the process. The whole procedure seemed to delight him, given the small whoops of glee he made when he remembered a particularly malevolent curse to incorporate into the charm. He felt invincible – no one had yet been able to stop him or even slow him down. And his enemies, as he conceived of them, were entirely in disarray with a variety of cuts, bruises, broken bones and teeth-chattering fear. Things were really working out.

He'd vanquished most of his foes and eliminated many of the people who might come by here and try to stop him. Osman was recovering, but Omar heard it was taking some time, which did not surprise him – he was surprised that he was recovering at all, but then he'd been so ambivalent about killing him it wasn't shocking to find this had been made manifest in his spells. He believed Deraman and Pak Lah had been shaken enough to stay away and tend to their own lives, and as for Maryam, who dared to poke her nose into his business… It made him furious to even think about her. The police and other bomoh were worthy opponents, but that this woman thought herself important enough to come after him was absolutely intolerable. He saved the bulk of his venom for her and her cousin, whom he also detested. After all, the police had a job to do, but what did these ladies think they were entitled to? He speeded up work on the jampi as he thought about it, but then purposely slowed himself to ensure no mistakes were made. This jampi was important.

He expected Deraman, and maybe another bomoh or two, to challenge him: after all, it would be a matter of professional pride after the healing ceremony gone terribly wrong. Omar did not want to take all the credit for that impressive show of power, though even when trying to be modest he had to ask who else could possibly have been involved? What other mortal human, at any rate? He had not, he told himself, meant to have poor Ramli die, nor had he done anything to bring it on. But forces can be unfettered, every so often, that cannot be controlled, and they can act on their own. Or so he told himself. He was not inordinately bothered; he never was at the collateral damage of his experiments with jampi. He had the attitude of a lab worker in an infectious disease clinic and expected some of his subjects would have to die in order to serve the greater good. That good being, of course, what Omar wanted at the time.

And what Omar wanted, deep down, was almost always the

same thing: that Jah return to him as she had been before and stay with him without slipping away. Occasionally he'd consider what his life might have been like had Jah not taken ill – would they have had children? Would he have been a contented village bomoh curing the sick and comforting the anxious? He believed so. He could, from time to time, fall into a reverie about this alternate life that seemed idyllic, surrounded by loving family and fond neighbours and friends. A bigger house, too, in which to keep those children and visiting relatives. A bustling and busy Jah, balancing childcare, maybe a *keropok* business (they were, after all, quite near to the coast and the fishermen, so keropok seemed a likely choice), cooking for her family and encouraging her husband. Perhaps a son who wanted to follow in his footsteps to become a bomoh as well, whom Omar could mentor and teach all he'd learned during his long and eventful life. It was a seductive and beautiful dream from which he had to wrench himself, lest returning to the real world become too painful.

He would only let himself think about that rarely, for when he did, he felt as though he floated away into this dream, with every detail lovingly imagined. It was far too dangerous to think about too much. It would take him away from the real world and leave him in some never land from which he could not emerge. No longer real, but not able to live in the fantasy either. He bent his head to his task and resolutely turned his mind away from his daydreams to the here and now.

Chapter XXX

Rahman led the junior members of the Kota Bharu police force to Kampong Laut, where they were joined by the local constables and a few men who wanted to help. He arranged them all around the land where the top spinning contest had taken place and directed them to dig until the entire area was completely turned over. It was hard work in the full sun, and Rahman asked Hassan's wife to deliver cold drinks continuously to keep the diggers healthy.

The men worked with enthusiasm, eager to see if anything could be found underground. Everyone at the contest had confirmed the ground had been swept and levelled and was perfectly clean and ready for the tops. But Rahman began to wonder whether anything had been buried under the carefully prepared surface, something that could affect the trajectory of the top. He'd said nothing about it until now, first doubting there was anything to find, then unwilling to speak up and open himself up to criticism. But his boss' weakness had made him less vulnerable to criticism, and now he no longer cared. He wanted every possibility explored.

The day wore on, and the previously flattened area now

looked like a buffalo wallow, with no real surface to speak of. Men stopped more often to take a drink, and most had shed their shirts, some wrapping them around their heads to keep the hair out of their eyes. Rahman started to dig himself, uncomfortable not taking part in what he'd ordered done. Better to work alongside his men and show his own commitment to the job.

His clothes were a mess, covered in dirt and sweat. Too late, he realized he should have worn something other than his uniform, which was not really designed for digging. And then he heard it. The clunk of a shovel hitting metal. It came from the corner of the 'platform'. And the man who'd found it was digging excitedly, helped by the men next to him. They pulled out a large metal sheet, which had been placed in the ground tilted rather than flat and was covered with signs they didn't understand. They were sure, however, they were meant to bring evil to the place they were in.

Rahman squatted next to the sheet, looking at it but not quite comprehending what it was supposed to do. 'It's there as a jampi,' said the man who'd found it. 'Maybe that's what made the top fly like it did.'

'How could it do that?' Rahman asked.

The man looked puzzled. 'I'm not sure, but what else would it be? And why would it be here, or all places?'

Another clunk made them turn, as Din, Rahman's junior policeman, hit another.

'Don't move it,' Rahman cried. 'Leave it where it is.'

He quickly walked over to Din's find. Here was the same metal sheet, tipped the same way the other had been, with slightly different but very similar markings. 'Maybe it's supposed to make the top move to that side. Isn't that where Hassan was sitting?' Din asked. 'Otherwise why place the sheets that way. I think we'll find more of them …'

Din was right, they found seven, all in that small space, all tipped toward the side where the top landed. 'How did it affect it?' Rahman wondered, as he had no doubt they helped guide the top to where Omar wanted it to go. Could the top have hit these sheets at the time? They weren't too far from the surface.

Rahman asked if anyone had been seen at the area before the contest, but no one was sure. It was open land after all, and no one was forbidden to come near it. Whoever came to bury the sheets wasn't noticed, so Rahman thought they'd probably done it at night. 'Unless they had a spell of invisibility,' Din suggested. Rahman didn't want to even think about that.

They pulled out the sheets, and nervously washed them off. 'I'm not that happy to get close to them,' Din told Rahman as he loaded them into the trunk of the police car. 'What if the jampi rubs off?'

He would have liked to scoff at Din: 'Rub off? How?' but he could not. Who knows what Omar might have accomplished? So he said nothing but continued carrying. They'd gone this far, there was no turning back.

He brought his findings to Osman first, as was only proper, but Osman could not give him the reaction he wanted. 'That's wonderful,' he said, trying to put some enthusiasm into his voice, but failing. 'Do you think Omar put it there?'

'Yes. Who else would do it?'

'Do you think he put it there to give some natural help to his jampi?' Osman wheezed. Weak he might be, but he came straight to the point.

'Yes,' Rahman nodded. 'I think this was supposed to do it. I'm not sure how exactly: maybe the top hit the sheet and went flying in the direction it was tipped? That's what I'm guessing. No one saw anything, or remembers anything, so maybe he buried them at night. Or,' he added morosely, 'maybe he did it in broad daylight, but no one saw him anyway. There's nothing I wouldn't believe right now.'

The news was greeted with far more animation at Maryam's house after dinner. 'What?' Maryam gasped. 'Plates of metal? Would they have made the …?'

'Believe what you want,' Rubiah said angrily. 'You think it wasn't jampi? Go ahead and try to make the top fly like that with just the sheets. Go ahead.'

'No, Mak Cik Rubiah, I don't mean that only the sheets …'

'That's exactly what you mean,' Rubiah would not be mollified. 'No one believed me when I said Omar did it, and now you're trying to figure out how it wouldn't be supernatural, as you say. Well, what do you think those sheets are, anyway, with all those symbols and writing all over them?'

'Of course,' Maryam agreed, 'they're more jampi but they're also more practical, you can see that. An assist, I would say.'

'Say anything,' Rubiah sniffed. 'I told you right at the beginning it was Omar and his black magic, and I still believe that. You can believe what you want.' She stopped looked at them.

Rahman and Maryam said nothing.

Deraman had no intention of leaving this alone. It wasn't just what happened at the ceremony, he'd actually lost a client whom he'd liked very much. There was a newly made widow and young children left behind, and Ramli needed to be avenged.

He needed allies but was reluctant to ask for any lest this turn out to be even more dangerous than he feared, and he feared quite a bit. Maryam, he'd heard from Pak Lah, was home nursing her injuries and could barely walk. Her cousin Rubiah would never take up this kind of mission without her. Osman too was injured, though Deraman believed he would insist on being involved, through professional pride if nothing else, but how much he'd be able to do was another issue. Rahman could be helpful, and he was in full command of his faculties. So, perhaps the police. Anyone else would be mad to participate, given the dangers and what they'd just witnessed, or at least had described to them in lurid detail.

He unconsciously straightened his shoulders where he sat and looked ahead instead of at the floorboards of his porch. He called Anim for coffee – courage often required a good deal of caffeine to keep it buoyant. His wife noticed his change of attitude immediately.

'You're ready now, aren't you?' she asked, placing the cup before him with a few curry puffs to keep up his strength. 'You're going ahead with it.' It wasn't a question.

He nodded. 'Then I'm helping you,' she said firmly. 'Don't say it!' She held up her hand to forestall argument. 'I know what you're going to say already, but it doesn't matter. This involves me too, now, and I want to be part of this.

'If it's dangerous for me it's dangerous for you, so let's not even discuss it. Tell me, what are we doing?'

Deraman had feared this but could not claim surprise either. Anim did not lack courage or conviction, and he realized there was no use in attempting to dissuade her. In fact, upon further consideration, he was proud of her, and truth be told, honoured to have her fighting with him. He smiled.

'Good,' she said, plumping herself down next to him. 'He needs to be stopped. What's our plan?'

'We don't have one yet,' Deraman admitted. 'But I'm thinking about it.'

'Pak Lah?' she asked. He nodded. 'Maryam?'

'I don't know if she can. I hear she can barely walk.'

Anim looked exasperated. 'Someone else can do the walking,' she said. 'We need Maryam's brain. And Rubiah's too. They can certainly plan.'

Deraman said nothing but began to suspect the project might be getting away from him.

'And the police as well. Osman might not be completely healed yet, but his men can help and Maryam's son-in-law, Rahman is it? He's very brave and smart, too. And his wife...'

'Do I get a say in any of this?'

'Do you disagree with any of it?'

'No.'

'Then?'

'Nothing.'

'Good.'

'We should go to Kampong Penambang then, since it will be

difficult for all of them on the other side of the river to travel. This way we can all sit together and make our plans.'

Deraman knew when it was time to agree.

Chapter XXXI

They were there for the big meeting, as Rubiah described it to herself. Everyone who was anyone in this case was gathered, with chairs having been brought in for those already injured. Maryam and Osman sat in state in large armchairs with everyone else gathered around them. Mamat and Abdullah volunteered their services, and though Yi attempted to volunteer his, he was unceremoniously dispatched to Ashikin's house to keep him out of trouble, as well as to help with childcare by taking Nuraini on a visit to the night market.

Deraman and Pak Lah began the discussions, as they were the (putative) leaders of the project. 'We need to stop him,' Pak Lah began.

***

'Do you mean kill him?' Osman interrupted.

Pak Lah was nonplussed. 'Well, I don't…not necessarily…I didn't want…'

'We'll have to,' Osman said bluntly, all traces of the diffident Perak boy erased. Perhaps it was his illness which forced him to get right to the point or made him too tired for dissimulation. 'How else can he be stopped? If he's alive, he's going to continue what he's doing, so as far as I can see there isn't any other alternative. And if so,' he continued relentlessly, 'we must admit it to ourselves right now, at the beginning, so we don't have any misunderstandings later. We will acknowledge what we're getting into, and what the result will be. And if anyone doesn't want to be part of it, which I can understand, announcing you're planning to kill someone isn't very comforting, then leave now. Let's not get to the end of our plan and then start hashing out whether or not killing him is the right thing to do.' He'd leaned forward during this unexpected lecture, and now fell back against the chair, exhausted. It might have been the longest and most impassioned speech he'd made since being carried out of Omar's house.

Azrina and Maryam looked at each other for a long moment. 'I think some of the younger people should leave now. Azrina, you're expecting and Aliza, I don't think you should be involved here. Not directly. It's too dangerous.'

Both Azrina and Aliza began to protest, but they were overruled by everyone in the room.

'I'd appreciate it if you could coordinate things,' Osman said softly, so that everyone leaned in to listen; his voice of just a moment ago already gone. 'Be behind the scenes. No need to be where he can see you.'

'But can't he see anyway? You know, his pelesit and all that, so we might as well…'

Aliza was frozen by a coordinated look from her mother, father and husband, and thought better of continuing her train of thought. There would be time later, she thought, to see how things could be managed. Right now, it was best to be discreet.

'Now, we're all agreed?' Osman retook the floor. 'It's murder.'

'It's retribution,' Rahman corrected him.

'We're planning to kill someone. Let there be no mistake about that.' Osman looked around the room as though he could look into each person's soul and determine whether or not they had the right stuff for this kind of job. 'It might keep you up at night in years to come if you really don't believe in what you're doing. We can't go on with main puteri after main puteri after this. So make sure.'

Rahman nodded quietly. He was in. Each person around the room nodded, there would be no tacit agreement here. Osman looked back at Pak Lah and gestured for him to continue.

'Are we too old for this?' Abdullah whispered to Mamat as Pak Lah began to talk.

'He tried to kill Maryam,' Mamat replied.

'Yeah, he did,' Abdullah said briefly, then crossed his arms and listened.

'… and Che Deraman and I are casting jampi to weaken him, though I must say we believe he's very strong indeed…'

'Maybe the strongest bomoh we've seen in all Kelantan, but of course for villainy …' Deraman interjected.

'… and therefore,' Pak Lah continued, 'we aren't completely confident we can really harm him. As Che Osman said, we need to make sure he stops this once and for all and I'm afraid that means killing him. Che Deraman and I have talked about whether there's any way to simply disarm him, so to speak, but we don't know of a way to deprive him of his power and his familiars and yet keep him alive. He'll always be a threat.'

'Can he send his familiars after us?' Rubiah asked.

'He already has and will continue to,' Pak Lah answered.

'Don't underestimate him,' Deraman said forcefully. 'You can't. He's even stronger than you think.' Everyone in the room looked at each other, growing fearful but determined not to show it.

Rahman looked particularly worried. He believed the final work would fall to him, and he would deal Omar's death blow. He hoped that wouldn't mean Omar would send his spirits and demons after his death. Was that possible? Didn't death end it all? He had to ask.

'Pak Lah,' he began. 'When Omar is dead, it's over, right? He isn't going to send anything to hurt us from the grave.'

'No. That can't happen.'

'But his pelesit may still live,' Deraman added in the interests of full disclosure. 'And we don't know what they might do, but they'll be looking for another master.'

'An evil one?' Rahman asked. 'Or could one of you take them over, maybe?'

'I don't know. I don't know them yet, so I don't know what's involved. It's a good point.'

Rahman wished it hadn't been. It gave him chills just thinking about those familiars wandering around looking for trouble. Give him a human adversary any day. He sidled over toward Osman and squatted down beside the chair.

'As policemen,' he began softly, 'this could be the end of our careers, you know. Killing someone, no matter what he's done. The courts would see it…'

'They'd see it as murder in cold blood.' Osman finished. 'I've thought of that.'

'And?'

'And can we leave him running around Kelantan killing people? Intimidating them? As policemen?'

'No. But we could arrest him instead of just…you know. Try to get him into court. And of course,' he added as a practical note, 'have the bomoh work on him. I completely agree with that. But if we were to shoot him, say, we could be the ones in jail.'

Osman nodded. 'You're right.'

'I suggest that we first bring him in. Keep him in jail. Charge him with Hassan's killing. And then, while we're doing that, Pak Lah and Deraman will have some time to do whatever it is they'll do. And if he attacks us, that will be a different story. But I can't see our best first move is to plan to kill him.'

Osman brought his head closer to Rahman's. 'Everyone is very wound up right now, and I think that's why they all agreed. Tonight, when they've had a chance to think about it, things will change, you'll see. It's a lot to kill a man.'

'So, should I bring him in?'

'Tomorrow. I'll come with you.'

They both turned to watch Pak Lah and Deraman debate the finer points of attacking Omar magically. Neither mentioned their conversation to anyone else.

Chapter XXXII

The next morning, Rahman and Din helped Osman into the car. Not an auspicious start for their raid, Rahman thought. Last night, Osman had seemed energized, stronger, more forceful. This morning he again seemed weak and lethargic.

Osman looked at him as if he'd read his mind. 'I'm better, even though I still look weak,' he said, and sighed. 'I'm determined, Rahman, and that will mean something. I will face him, and I will win.'

Rahman attempted to look far more convinced than he was and prayed that Osman was telling the truth. He'd hate to wrestle Omar into the car with only Din for help. He'd suggested taking several more of their men, even in another car, but Osman was immovable: he wanted this to stay small. Rahman wondered if he wanted to keep the witnesses to his possible collapse to a minimum, and then discarded the thought as disloyal. Nevertheless...

They pulled up to the village of Cabang Tiga. Named only for the three way cross road on which it sat, it was more of a traffic marker than a real kampong, but it did have that coffee shop at the end of the dirt track that led to Omar's house. The owner nodded to them and wished them good morning in tones which said good luck. Could anyone look at them and know what they were planning? He hoped not.

They walked down the path, which seemed shorter in the daylight, with Osman hanging on to Rahman's arm, and Din discretely supporting him on the other side. They brushed aside the plants which had grown up in the yard and approached the house. At the bottom of the steps to Omar's house, Osman called out in a strong voice, 'Che Omar, are you here?'

It was a courtesy only, since Omar was sitting on the porch working away, and Jah sat in the corner. He looked up, seeming only mildly surprised.

'Ah, Police Chief Osman, you're here. Come on up. Feeling better, I see.'

He smiled at them, which was bone-chilling. Much like watching a shark smile, and with the same warmth.

Osman took the steps slowly, with both Rahman and Din behind him with their hands on his back. At the top, he did not immediately sit down, but stood and looked down at Omar, who had not risen.

'You've been busy,' Osman opened.

'Have I?'

'I heard about Kampong Laut and the exorcism. People will be talking about it for years.'

'I heard the same,' Omar said. 'It's the talk of Kelantan. I wasn't there though, so there isn't much I can add to the conversation.' He waved his arm in invitation for them to all sit down. Rahman thought it odd they would look like they were visiting when they'd come to arrest him, but he'd let Osman take the lead. Unless Osman fainted, in which case he would take over and drag Omar down the stairs by the back of his shirt.

'Didn't you know about it?'

'Not till afterward. You know, we're a bit isolated out here.'

'People are talking about you being the owner of all the spirits who turned up and killed Ramli and hurt so many other people.'

'Ah, people talk. You know how it is.'

'I think it's more than talk, now.'

'Do you? And why?'

'You've got such strong magic, everyone knows it,' Osman continued. Rahman felt he'd let the initiative get away from him and was allowing Omar to direct the conversation. He could not interrupt his boss, so he sat quietly with rising anxiety.

'You don't really believe all this stuff,' Omar said again, looking down at what he'd been working on. 'You're from the West Coast, where people are more modern than they are here. What would people in Perak say if they knew you were here to arrest me for witchcraft. It sounds crazy, doesn't it?'

'Not to anyone who knows you.' Osman seemed to be getting tired again.

Rahman decided it was time to get him back to Kota Bharu. 'We'd like you to come back to the station with us,' he began in his most commanding voice. 'We'll talk there. Are you ready?'

Omar seemed surprised by such directness. 'Back to Kota Bharu? I have things to do here.'

'The police are asking you to come with them, Che Omar. It's not an invitation to a party. Let's go.'

He stood up and Din followed. Osman stayed sitting rather

than waste his fading strength. Omar began to look concerned.

'I can't go. My wife is here. Who will take care of her?'

'We'll ask your neighbours.'

'They won't know what to do.'

'Che Omar, let's go.' Rahman took a hold of his arm and pulled him to his feet.

'She'll die!' Omar shouted, loud enough for the whole village to hear. 'You're leaving her to die.' He began to twist out of Rahman's grasp, who tightened his hold.

'Shall we take her with us?' he asked Omar. 'That way she'd be…'

'No!' he cried, losing his control. 'I don't want her there. You can't take me away; you can talk to me here.' His neighbour had come to see what was happening and causing all the noise.

'Leave me!' It was now a shrill scream, and Rahman was shocked at how quickly things had gone wrong. 'You're killing my wife! You're demons and you're trying to kill my wife!'

Omar's neighbours may have thought him crazy as well as dangerous, but they were sympathetic to his plight when the police tried to drag him off. 'Hey! What's this about?' the man demanded, looking up at them from the overgrown yard.

'We're bringing him in for questioning,' Rahman replied, wishing again they'd brought more men with them. Din was already hyperventilating.

'Why? What's he done?'

'There's a long list which I can't tell you right now. Just let me say this has been long overdue…'

Osman toppled over on his side, and Rahman let go of

Omar to attend to him. Omar ran down the stairs and held on to his neighbour's arms. 'Help me!' he begged. The man seemed frightened, as if he'd never expected to have Omar touching him when he'd intervened. Things had suddenly gotten more serious than he'd wanted. He started to back away, but Omar dug his nails into the man's arms and would not release him.

'Let me go,' his neighbour said, a note of incipient hysteria creeping into his voice. He ripped his arms away from Omar in a mighty heave, which left them scratched and bleeding. He stared at his arms and then at Omar.

'What are you doing? *Seperti anjing melentang denai*: like a dog crossing the track of game. You've lost control of yourself. Stop!'

Omar tried to throw himself against his neighbour, who backed away, holding his hands in front of him to ward off any further mauling. Osman seemed to have lost consciousness, and Omar seemed to have lost his mind. It was worse than Rahman ever imagined.

'Din! Go to the main road and call the station. Get our guys here as fast as possible.' He was about to add another comment about emergencies, but Din had already taken off, sprinting down the dirt road. Rahman let the neighbour deal with Omar, taking a bit of satisfaction knowing he'd gotten himself into this, and would now be left to get himself out. He tried to bring Osman back, but he wasn't responding.

Din pounded back down the road at top speed, followed by the local constable and all the men who'd been sitting around the coffee shop. The policeman helped Rahman carry Osman down the stairs to their waiting car. The other men restrained Omar, perhaps with more enthusiasm than was strictly necessary. The first neighbour began declaiming loudly about how he'd been attacked, and Omar was becoming the target of some very pointed looks, quite a change from his neighbour's initial instinct to protect him.

Rahman sent Din to sit with Osman and came back with the local policeman to sort out the developing riot. Rahman wasn't sure whether it would be pro or anti Omar, but was convinced Omar would be part of it. Right now, he was hanging from the arms of two sturdy men, gasping for breath and beginning to whine. Another man was applying water to the neighbour's badly scratched arms. Now that Rahman could take a look at them, they looked terrible, already swollen and somehow dirty. Clearly, they were also painful, as the man was growing pale and tensed, asking for his wife and maybe a doctor. No one knew how these cuts were so bad so quickly, but it didn't look natural. And now murmurings began about witchcraft and black magic and murder.

The man's wife arrived from next door with cloths and salve, took one look at her husband's scratches, and began berating Omar as a wild animal for attacking her husband when he was trying to help. She was encouraged by the crowd, which was growing larger as other neighbours arrived, drawn by the noise and the police. The tide had now turned against Omar rather than the police, and Rahman realized his role was now becoming one of protecting Omar, though he did briefly consider letting the mob do what they wanted with him. He and the constable grabbed Omar under the arms and began frog marching him to the car, when they were met by the contingent from Kota Bharu. Rahman handed Omar over to them and tried to disperse the crowd, which had grown uglier and more aggrieved.

The man's wife was still orating, but he now seemed sicker, slick with sweat and beginning to falter. Rahman staunched the flow of her rhetoric to ask if he should be taken to the hospital, motioning two of his men to bring him to their car. His wife followed behind.

'He shouldn't be allowed to live here,' one man averred. 'Look what he's done to Awang who was only trying to help him.' Other men agreed, milling around angrily, looking at Omar's house.

The police tried to disperse everyone, and while they initially walked away, they never left the area. Rahman left several policemen there to watch things while he went to take Osman to Pak Lah.

When it seemed all had calmed down, the police began to make their way back, stopping for a well-deserved coffee at the shop on the main road.

'Quite the excitement,' the owner commented, still seeing groups of men milling about. 'He isn't too popular around here.'

'People are afraid, right?' one of the men asked.

The owner nodded. 'Black magic,' he said sagely. 'And maybe a little crazy.' He looked quickly over his shoulder, then realized Omar was not in the kampong. 'I guess he can't hear me now,' he said with more bravado than he felt.

As they rose from their stools, they noticed a bit of smoke from down the dirt road, and immediately feared the worst. When they arrived at Omar's house, it was already catching fire while the crowd stood silently and watched. 'It's better he stay away,' one of the men said quietly.

No one in the crowd remembered Jah, who remained still and silent until the end, never moving or even seeming to notice that she was burning with her home.

Chapter XXXIII

Osman had been brought back to his quarters and was attended by Azrina and Pak Lah. Azrina had kept up a brave face up to now, but she was beginning to crack. She wondered whether Osman would ever fully recover or would instead be a ghostly presence for the rest of their lives together. It would leave her to raise their child alone, and the very thought left her breathless. Would she have to move them all back to her parents' home in Perak? Would Osman be left unable to work or maybe even get out of bed? She began to wring her hands and prepared to cry.

'He needs you to be strong,' Pak Lah commanded her, not taking his eyes off Osman. 'You can't fall apart now.' He lifted Osman's eyelids and whatever he saw did not seem to please him greatly. He'd never used so many jampi at one time before, but then he'd never fought anything like this either, and he certainly hoped never to do so again. He was too old for this.

'Will he wake up today?' she asked anxiously.

Pak Lah looked doubtful. 'I don't know. I might know in a bit. Can you please make some coffee for me? I need to concentrate and that would be helpful.'

Azrina dutifully left, and Pak Lah allowed himself a small sigh of relief. This jampi would require some manhandling, and it was best Azrina not be present for it. He began getting his pins ready.

***

At the police station, things were calming down. Omar had been a guest at the station before, and they all expected nothing but trouble from him. He sat in the 'interrogation' room, at a table with tea and some dry biscuits (somehow even criminal investigations required some snacks), looking both sly and unhappy. He had not answered any of their questions except with another question, which was beginning to get on Rahman's nerves. Perhaps a night in the cells might make him more amenable to answers, although Rahman wasn't sure Omar cared much about that.

He leaned back in his chair, Din sitting behind him, both eager to hear the questioning and afraid to be in the same room as Omar, who was looking even more disreputable than usual. He seemed to have identified the weak link however, and continued to shoot glances at Din, and worse yet, smile at him, which kept the young man completely off balance.

'You have nothing on me,' Omar said. It had taken them a while to get him calmed down after taking him out of Cabang Tiga, and Rahman had been unable to stop himself from calling Omar's attention to how much his neighbours disliked him. Omar tried to wave it away as of no account, but Rahman thought it might be an opening to crack Omar's self-control. Now, however, he was drinking tea and being quiet, having some amusement in intimidating Din and no doubt convincing himself that his village did not hate him quite as much as it seemed.

The cars returned from Cabang Tiga, with soot smeared and dejected police, dreading telling Rahman what had happened. He heard their entrance and left Omar with Din, silently apologizing to him, and went out to see them.

'What happened to you?' he asked, puzzled.

'There was a fire.'

'Where?'

'At the house.'

'What?'

'We thought everything was over, and people were starting to leave and everything, so we thought we could leave also. We had a cup of coffee at the stall, and then saw smoke. So we went back down the road as fast as we could and someone had set fire to the house.'

'What?'

He nodded sadly. 'I know. The neighbours were all standing around very quietly, watching it burn. It didn't take too long, a small place and the fire didn't spread, though it would have served them right if it had. They all seemed sort of relieved. '

'It was a riot.'

'Kind of. Anyway, after the fire was out we wanted to make sure there wasn't some evidence left...'

'Evidence?'

'Yes, and so we looked, and you could smell it.'

Rahman had a very bad feeling about this. 'What?'

'His wife was in there.'

'Alamak!'

'Everyone was shocked. I think the crowd was happy to have burned it down but when they realized they'd killed someone, well…'

'Do you know who started it?'

He shook his head. 'No one would talk. I think it wasn't one person you know; it was the whole mob. I've never seen anything like that. They're taking what's left to bury.' He hung his head. 'I wish we hadn't left but I didn't think they'd do anything like this. I really didn't.'

'This whole thing is a disaster,' Rahman said, sitting down and burying his face in his hands. 'How did it go downhill so quickly?'

'They hate him,' the officer replied. 'That's the whole thing.'

'But his wife?'

'I don't think anyone knew she was there. You'd all gone, and she didn't move or make a sound. I can't…'

'Believe it,' Rahman finished for him. He stared straight ahead, trying to absorb all that had happened since this morning. A year's worth of disaster in just a couple of hours. He even felt sorry for Omar when he heard this news. He'd be bereft. Or furious, you couldn't really tell with him. Rahman had the overpowering desire to have this whole day never have happened, but there he was, and there was no way but forward.

Omar seemed to have sensed something. He pushed Din out

of the way and walked out of the room, seeing the group looking dishevelled and disheartened. 'What's this?' he asked.

No one answered. Rahman didn't know what to say, and the others had no intention of taking on this explanation. 'Go back into the room,' Rahman said softly.

'What happened?' Omar repeated. 'Tell me.'

'Later.'

'Now.'

Rahman took a deep breath. Might as well get it over with. 'Che Omar,' he began formally, 'it appears there was a fire in your kampong, and unfortunately your house was burned.'

'The whole house?'

The soot covered policeman nodded.

'Everything in it?'

'I'm sorry,' Rahman said.

'Jah?'

Rahman looked up at him and said nothing.

'Jah?' he began to scream. 'Is she dead?'

Rahman had the sense he was making a hash out of breaking the news to Omar. He mumbled 'Yes.'

'They burned her in the house?' The whites were beginning to show under his eyes, and his teeth somehow looked more prominent. 'They never took her out of the house?'

'I don't think they knew she was in there. I'm sure they're very sorry.' It seemed so inadequate.

Omar burst into sobs, crouching against the wall. The right thing would be to sit next to him and put a brotherly arm around his shoulder, but no one wanted to even get close to him, less still touch him. They stood awkwardly in front of him, offering no comfort, though each believed he should.

'Come, Che Omar,' Rahman finally said, 'let's get up…'

'Stay away from me,' Omar hissed, though Rahman had made no move towards him.

'I will, but please let's move to a chair and have some tea.' It sounded lame even to him.

'Tea?' In spite of himself, Omar sounded amused. 'Is that what you think will help?'

'No, but at least…'

'You'll suffer for this,' Omar assured him, and Rahman absolutely believed him. 'But first the people who did this to my poor Jah. Who never hurt anyone! Never wanted to! And they killed her.'

They stood silent, ashamed. He was right.

'How will I live without her?' he asked abruptly. 'She was my life. She was all I lived for. There's no point to me being alive now.' He began to sob again. 'They will all pay for this.'

'You're very upset, Che Omar,' Rahman began again. He turned and whispered to one of the men to get Pak Lah, who was in the quarters with Osman. 'Of course you are, but we need to put our trust in God…'

Omar continued to cry and held up his had to signal Rahman to be quiet, and he complied.

Pak Lah came, looking concerned. 'I heard, Omar, about what happened. I'm so sorry.'

He stopped crying and looked up malevolently at Pak Lah. 'Are you?'

'Yes I am. She is a loss.'

'I only wanted to help her.'

'Of course.'

'I only wanted her to come back to me. That's all I wanted.'

'Were you using other people to do that?'

Omar was far past caring. 'I chose Jah. Other people, well, if I need something from them to give to Jah then I will do it.'

'Even if it kills them.'

He shrugged. 'People die. We're all going to die. Sooner or later.'

'Yes, but...'

'Don't lecture me!' Omar's temper flared. 'Are you now going to tell me how to do what I do? Tell me what's moral and what isn't? I have magic stronger than anything you've ever imagined.'

'I'm sure that's true,' Pak Lah admitted.

'I studied it. I worked at it. I made it my life. But all to help her, that's what it was for. I had to try out my spells, to see if they worked. I couldn't try them on her, she could get hurt.'

'Other people got hurt.'

Omar shrugged, completely unconcerned. 'I will make you all suffer as I have.'

'Don't say that.'

Omar looked up and gave Pak Lah a smile so purely evil everyone in the room stepped back. 'You're afraid,' he said happily, and slowly began rising.

Pak Lah stretched out a hand to help him up. Omar grasped it and dug his fingers deep into Pak Lah's hands. Pak Lah yelped in pain and surprise.

'Yes, how do you like this?' Omar asked.

Pak Lah tried to draw himself back, but he was held tight. Omar pulled himself up, tearing at Pak Lah's flesh, leaving long gashes, but still he did not let go. Pak Lah looked down in horror at his shredded hands and recognized these as the same cuts he saw on Maryam's legs. Omar must have been there, in Kampong Laut, somehow.

'You see now,' Omar said happily. 'You will never heal. Neither will Maryam. Look at the rest of your life!'

Pak Lah could still not extricate himself. 'I won't let you go. I know you'll want to kill me, aren't I right? I know. But here you are, you can't even move your hands,' he taunted him. 'You can't get free. I have you for now, and maybe forever. How will you be rid of me? You won't.' With a wild cry he took one of his hands away from Pak Lah's, and grabbed his shoulder instead. Pak Lah shouted in pain.

'Hurts, doesn't it? It probably hurt Jah too, but she couldn't make a sound. All she could do was just burn, silently. Be grateful you can at least cry out.'

Just as it had with Omar's neighbour, Pak Lah's hands began to swell and burn. His shoulder was now on fire. Rahman and his men pulled themselves out of the trance they were in and grabbed Omar, trying to draw him off Pak Lah, but he held fast. Omar did not even fight them, he went limp in their grasp and moved his arms to Pak Lah's neck, who shrieked, and things began to go dark. Rahman tried desperately to peel Omar off his victim, but Omar did not care. He hung on, happy to have Pak Lah at his mercy, another soul in exchange for Jah's. In desperation, Rahman punched him as hard as he could in the shoulder, and Omar let go and fell back, hitting his head on a desk with a hollow thud, and sliding to the floor.

Chapter XXXIV

Pandemonium reigned in the police station, with two bomoh stretched on the floor, and Pak Lah bleeding copiously. He was conscious again but knew he would not survive this.

'The ambulance is coming,' Rahman whispered urgently. 'It will be right here. Just hang on. He can't hurt you anymore.'

Pak Lah smiled and shook his head. 'I'm too old for this,' he said out loud, after having thought it so often. 'I can't take it anymore.'

'Don't say that,' Rahman had tears in his eyes. 'It will be better, you'll see.' He wanted to hold Pak Lah's hand but feared to touch it lest he cause still more pain. 'We need you!'

Pak Lah smiled briefly. 'I'm so tired,' he said.

***

It was a while before anyone looked at Omar, lying on the floor of the station. They were far more concerned with Pak Lah, who they did want to lose, than Omar, who in fact they did. Nevertheless, they did their duty, and as soon as Pak Lah had been cared for, they turned to Omar.

Though he lay there without moving, they were still afraid to come to near. Rahman craned his neck to see him, though there was nothing blocking his view. If he got too close to Omar, would he suddenly rise up and hook his poisonous fingernails into Rahman's flesh, ripping his body as he dragged them down his arms? Rahman thought he might live with that picture for the rest of his life.

They all stood far enough away that even if Omar opened his eyes and began to move they could easily evade him, and no one volunteered to get any closer. Eventually Rahman gingerly stepped forward, wishing he had a long stick with which to poke the bomoh so he wouldn't need to touch him. It was like circling a wounded cobra.

When at last he touched his face, it seemed he was dead. He took some courage from that and put his hand on Omar's chest to check for breathing but found none. It would have been nice if anyone in the room had felt anything but relief, but there was nothing else.

'I think he's dead,' Rahman said, trying to keep his voice steady. 'I wish I were sorry about that, but I'm not.' It saved the group having to undertake murder, and that in itself was a blessing. There would no doubt be an investigation, but Rahman was confident it would be termed an accident which occurred while the victim was wildly attacking an innocent man and put down to a judicious use of force.

'Can you call the morgue?' Rahman asked one of the men behind him. Better that Omar be handled by someone who didn't know him and therefore would not be unravelled by his corpse.

Not one of the policemen present could comfortably have done it, and Rahman would not ask them to do something he couldn't do himself. 'I'm going to see the Chief,' he announced, and walked to the quarters behind the station.

He entered the house to find Azrina flitting nervously back and forth. 'What happened? I could hear something...I didn't want to leave Osman alone, you know...Pak Lah, is he alright? I was afraid, I'll admit it, but I couldn't leave him alone and helpless. So I stayed here...'. Her speech tapered off and she looked pleadingly at Rahman.

'Everything's fine now,' he said, not quite accurately. 'There's nothing to worry about.'

'What happened?'

'Omar is dead.' Maybe he should have prepared her, but he was suddenly exhausted. 'Pak Lah, well, he's hurt, and he's been sent to the hospital.'

'I'm glad he's dead,' Azrina said firmly. 'Maybe we can go back to our normal lives now.'

'I know,' Rahman agreed. 'You know, his house was burned down earlier.'

'I heard.'

'And his wife was burned with it.'

She put her hand up to her mouth. 'Alamak! Didn't anyone know she was there?'

'I don't think so. That is, they wanted to burn down his house, but I don't think they were trying to kill his wife. It's just that...I don't think they knew she was there, and you know she doesn't move or speak so there were no sounds that could tell them she was there. Our guys only found out after the house came down.'

'The poor woman. How horrible!'

'Yes, it was, poor thing. What a pity.' He was silent for a moment. 'I think that's why Omar was ready to die. If he weren't, he wouldn't have. He had such strong magic. But when he found out Jah was dead, he couldn't go on. I think he tried to take Pak Lah with him, but I hope that isn't the case.'

'Is he badly hurt?'

Rahman nodded. 'It looked like it.'

'Maybe Osman will get well now that Omar's gone.'

'Do you think?'

'I hope so. Can his magic continue without him?'

Rahman shook his head. 'I don't know much about it. I really don't want to know. I guess I should let Deraman know.'

'Thank you for telling me.'

'You're welcome. Please *kirim salaam*, send my regards, to Che Osman. I'll stop in tomorrow to check on him.'

And with that, he went home.

Chapter XXXIV

Deraman was speechless, a condition in which he did not often find himself. Sitting on his porch next to Anim, he goggled at Rahman as though unable to comprehend what he'd just said.

'So, Jah was just burned?'

Rahman nodded sadly. 'Yes, it's a shame.'

'Maybe not,' Anim piped up. They both turned to look at her. 'I'm just being realistic,' she explained. 'She wanted to leave this world, you know. And without Omar, what would she do? Who would take care of her? Would she be better off starving to death silently?'

She waited for an answer but received none. 'Of course not,' she answered herself. 'No, without Omar, it's a blessing for Jah. Though of course,' she hurriedly added, 'the way she died is horrible. No one would want that. But that she died at all? Well...'

'I guess you're right,' Deraman muttered, unwilling to discuss this proposition at length.

'Do you think everyone who's been hurt by Omar will get better now?' Rahman asked. 'A lot of people have been wounded or cut and aren't healing,' he said, thinking of his mother-in-law, 'and I wondered if with him gone, would his magic go with him?'

Deraman furrowed his brow. 'It should. After all, it was his strength which kept these spells so potent.'

'And his pelesit,' Rahman pressed on. 'What will happen to them? Are they just wandering around now with no one to own them?'

Deraman nodded. 'I believe they are.'

'So what will happen? I'd hate for another person to take them on and continue Omar's...work. Could we stop that? Could you take them?'

'I've never wanted any,' Deraman told him. 'I don't want to have that kind of thing with me.'

'But what will we do about it?' Rahman was becoming anxious just thinking about it. Those spirits wandering around the kampong of Kelantan, raising hell on their own with no one controlling them. And they'd been taught by Omar and so would have a large repertoire of wickedness from which to pick.

'I'm not sure.'

'Don't they need a master?'

Deraman gave Rahman a distinctly annoyed look, wishing he would drop it, but seeing now he would not let it go. 'They should have one, this is what I've heard.'

'Otherwise, they'll just start attacking everyone,' Rahman continued.

'When did you learn so much about them?' Deraman asked tartly. 'Perhaps you would like to take it over.'

'Now, Deraman,' Anim began, 'he's only concerned, as are we all.'

'I know that, but what will I do with these creatures? I've no use for this kind of thing, especially if they've belonged to Omar. God only knows what kind of things they've been taught.'

'Can they be untaught?'

Deraman threw up his hands in frustration. 'I must speak with Pak Lah when he's better,' he said, trying his best to end the conversation right there. 'I'm not the pelesit expert, and what's more, I don't want to be. Do you understand that?'

Rahman nodded, but the problem kept coming back to him. 'But do you think people will start to heal now?'

'Yes,' said Anim, earning a surprised look from her husband. 'I think we all will start to improve now that he's gone. Maybe even his pelesit will follow him into hell. I hope so, you know. They don't belong on this earth.' She looked determined.

'Well, if everyone knows better than I do,' Deraman said in the beginning of a sulk, 'then I'm not sure my opinion is that necessary.'

'Stop it,' Anim said sharply, surprising Rahman and her husband both. 'This is too big to be personal. We've got to make sure that these fiends are put away where they won't come back. They say it's mostly women who keep pelesit, don't they?'

'Stop,' her husband commanded. 'Those are witches. Don't even think about it?'

'We could bottle them up...'

'No.' Deraman said. 'No, we cannot.' He rose from the porch. 'I'm going to Kota Bharu to see Pak Lah.'

'I'll come with you,' Anim said calmly. 'Let's go.'

***

Rahman returned home to an uproar he could not quite figure out. How had the news spread so quickly to Kampong Penambang? But it seemed as if his whole family had some abbreviated version of what happened. Even his parents had come to Maryam's house to find out the details.

Contravening all precepts of Malay courtesy, Aliza rushed down the stairs of her parents' house to greet Rahman and threw her arms around his neck. 'I was so worried about you! Are you OK? We've heard about Omar.'

'What have you heard?' he asked, reluctant to break the embrace. 'I'm fine, see? I'm here.'

'I heard Pak Lah was hurt.'

'Where have you heard all this?'

Aliza shrugged. 'Everyone's talking. Ashikin heard it in the market and came right back to tell us. But other people in the kampong already knew.'

It was like osmosis: there were no secrets in a Malay village. He knew that, and yet was surprised anew each time the efficiency of the grapevine was proved again.

'I went to see Deraman to tell him what happened,' Rahman continued. 'I asked him about the familiars and all that Omar would have had. Where will they go now?'

'Can't they go with him, wherever that is?' she asked. 'Or with Jah? Maybe they were hers in the beginning.'

'Can they just go with him? Could it be that easy?'

Aliza shrugged. 'I don't know. I don't care.'

By now their families were calling down for them to come up to the house and tell them what had happened. He smiled at Aliza; it was wonderful to have someone like her to come home to after such an experience.

They walked up the steps to be greeted by everyone asking questions at once, pushing a cup of coffee into his hands and cakes on the table in front of him. He was very nearly wrestled into his chair. Maryam began the interrogation, somehow seeming much stronger and more in control than he'd seen her since the disaster that was the main puteri.

'He's dead, isn't he?'

Rahman nodded. 'He attacked Pak Lah.' There was a collective intake of breath. 'Scratched him down the arms, which gave him the same cuts you have,' he nodded at his mother-in-law. 'And they started to swell up immediately.'

'Alamak!' she said softly.

'Yes. We pulled him off Pak Lah and he hit his head on a table. He was dead.'

'He must have wanted to die,' Ashikin contemplated. 'Otherwise he might not have. His spirit was so strong. So ... unholy.' She shuddered delicately. 'I'm glad he's dead.'

'And Pak Lah?' Maryam asked.

Rahman sighed. 'I don't know. He's in the hospital, I think.'

'Will he be alright?'

'I don't know,' he repeated. 'I haven't heard anything. I did stop to see how Osman was doing. He'd been with Osman when we brought Omar in.

'They burned his house down in Cabang Tiga.'

'Who?' Maryam leaned forward.

'His neighbours. There was a big crowd when we went to bring him back to the police station. When we got him out, they turned ugly.' He thought for a moment. 'He attacked one of his neighbours with his nails, his claws, really. That guy's also in the hospital.'

Rubiah shook her head disapprovingly. 'Like an animal.'

'And Jah is dead.'

They were silent. 'How?'

'She was in the house when they burned it.'

They remained silent. Finally, Maryam said, 'Poor thing. Did they know?'

'I don't think so. She was sitting in the corner, like she did. Like a statue. When we left I don't think anyone else saw her. And she didn't move or make a sound the whole time.

Aliza winced. 'Oh no.'

'Maybe it's for the best,' Ashikin said practically. 'Maybe that's why Omar was ready to go, and besides, who would take care of her while he was gone?'

'That's what people are saying.' Rahman said gloomily. 'That it was meant to be.'

Ashikin nodded, pleased to be confirmed in her opinion.

'What a horror,' Rubiah said. 'I knew it would be. I had a feeling.'

Maryam forbore to comment. 'Will I be getting better now? Will everyone who was hurt by him be getting better? Osman?'

'I don't know that either.' Rahman said. 'I may know more tomorrow. But now, I've got to go home.'

Rubiah hurried back from the kitchen, brandishing a banana leaf package. 'Dinner,' she informed him.

Chapter XXXV

Maryam was back in the market, where she belonged. After Omar's death, the cuts on her legs, as deep and vicious as they were, began to heal. Slowly at first, and then, all of a sudden, they were gone.

Her legs no longer hurt, and more perplexing, the geese no longer attacked her. They seemed to recognize her again and knew that she provided their food. No longer was she surrounded when she came down the stairs or pursued into the yard. She wondered if they had mistaken her for Omar or sensed the evil present in her legs and therefore tried to get her out of their territory. Now that she was well, they were hardly cuddly, but neither were they trying to kill her. She was amazed at their perspicacity in this matter, given their stubborn obliviousness in so much else.

Osman too had recovered quickly once Omar had left this world. His lethargy evaporated, he returned to work and to Azrina as the husband she'd had before. What's more, word began to trickle in from Rantau Panjang about how strict Osman had been about smuggling questionable entertainment. He had an iron will, it was said, and simply would not tolerate it. Not, emphatically, that he interfered with rice coming in from Thailand, which would have been wrong. But blue movies would not be allowed. The Chinese Merchants Association had done itself proud.

In his newfound energy he threw himself into baby planning and insisted Azrina rest when she returned from teaching. True, he did not take over the cooking, but he was a master at picking up takeout from the market, thereby saving Azrina from having to consider feeding them. He conferred with Maryam and Rubiah about finding someone to help in the house, and they were both delighted with the way he took over the task of ensuring Azrina could relax. Unfortunately, their own husbands did not compare well in this particular arena, but Maryam tried to write it off as being a different time. Rubiah was not so sure, but what was there to argue? She preferred the explanation that Osman's brush with death and the black arts had made him more sensitive and appreciative of his wife now, in a way that men who had not believed they were about to die could not understand. Not that she would wish such an experience on anyone, though it might prove character enhancing for many.

And although some of those involved wanted to cling to a natural explanation, involving the metal plates buried under the ground, tipping the top towards the side where the luckless Hassan sat, Rubiah was not one of them. She never doubted the whole affair was brought about by black magic and black magic alone. Surely Omar was malicious enough, and strong enough, to carry it off, even if there were others too afraid to see it. It annoyed Rubiah no end to hear anyone mention those metal sheets. She'd told them, she couldn't count the times, but they looked for a reason less frightening. Let them, she thought. It was the weaker alternative: Rubiah, at least, was unafraid to look unpleasant truths in the face, and thereby understand exactly what happened. Metal plates, indeed!

Pak Lah lived, but in what appeared to be a diminished state. He had come home, and was physically recovered, but would no longer practice as a bomoh. In this he was encouraged, even commanded, by his wife, who made clear to Maryam that Pak Lah was now retired. 'It's time for him to enjoy his life, not battle with the likes of Omar,' she told her. 'He came way too close to dying for my taste, and he's an older man. It took everything out of him! Even though the cuts healed, he's not back to himself. He doesn't have a lot of energy. I want things calm for him. Quiet. We're going to visit our daughter in Pasir Mas and stay with our grandchildren,' she said with determination. 'There are other bomoh in the world. My husband has done all he could.' She looked at Maryam as if daring her to disagree, but Maryam did not. She was right. Pak Lah had earned his rest. He'd been heroic, and Maryam was deeply grateful to him. No one could ask any more.

She saw him occasionally, sitting on his porch, sipping coffee, reading the paper, looking completely content. 'Do you miss it at all?' she asked him once.

He smiled at her and shook his head. 'I'm too old for that now,' he said. 'That whole thing with Omar just about killed me. I thought it had. No more. It's time for younger men to take over. Deraman is an excellent bomoh,' he said, nodding at her. 'You should use him if you need anything. I'm retired. Ask my wife,' he added with a smile. 'Do you want any coffee?'

She politely declined.

And, just as Ashikin had predicted, Aliza and Rahman were going to have a baby. Once Ashikin had said it, Aliza had sort of known it was happening, though the details were still a little vague. No more. They were only six months away from becoming parents.

Acknoweldgements

I would like to thank Bonnie Tessler and Zdena Nemckova for their help in reading drafts and proof reading. Thanks to Shahmim Dhilawallah, Puteh Shaharizan Shaari and Ashikin Mohd. Ali Flindall for their insights into Malay culture. And to all of them for their unfailing encouragement.

To my daughters, Jerushah Ismail and Arielle Fields, my deepest thanks and love for you just being there, and to my new grandson Philip who gives us all such joy.

And of course, to Philip Tatham, my publisher, whose help and confidence has been such a gift.

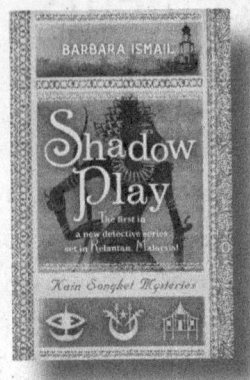